CHANCE ENCOUNTER

Rick Tremaine is determined to discover what really killed his brother, a junior swimming champion, who died suddenly at a Melbourne health and fitness centre. Though he trusts no-one at the complex, Rick is increasingly drawn to Tessa Raymond, the assistant manager, and confides to her his suspicions that performance-enhancing drugs are being sold on the premises. Shocked, Tessa sets out to disprove Rick's allegation, but her investigation leads her into mortal danger . . .

JO JAMES

CHANCE ENCOUNTER

Complete and Unabridged

LINFORD
Leicester

First published in Great Britain in 2002

First Linford Edition
published 2002

British Library CIP Data

James, Jo
  Chance encounter.—Large print ed.—
Linford romance library
  1. Love stories
  2. Large type books
  I. Title
  823.9'2 [F]

  ISBN 1–8439–5052–9

Published by
F. A. Thorpe (Publishing)
Anstey, Leicestershire

Set by Words & Graphics Ltd.
Anstey, Leicestershire
Printed and bound in Great Britain by
T. J. International Ltd., Padstow, Cornwall

This book is printed on acid-free paper

1

Tessa looked around the coffee shop. She was in luck. There was one spare table with a sunny outlook, facing the Esplanade. Perhaps her day was about to improve. She hurried across to it, but a waiter intercepted her.

Raising his arms, he said, 'Sorry, very sorry, Miss Raymond. It's reserved. You take the spare chair at the table over there, yes?'

She followed his glance to the darkest corner of the café.

'No, Angelo. It's gloomy and it's occupied. Where does it say this one's reserved, anyway?' she said testily.

He waved his hands.

'Too busy, too busy. I mean to do it, but it's hectic since twelve o'clock. You ask the gentleman over there. He be happy to share. If you like, I ask. He come in regular.'

She groaned. A regular probably meant an old boy with nothing else to do but sit around waiting for someone to happen along for a chat. She wasn't in the mood for a chat! After Darren's odious behaviour, and the argument which followed, the only company she trusted was her own. But her need for an intake of caffeine was even greater. One small blessing, though, the table's occupier had his head buried in a newspaper.

'Thanks, Angelo, but I am capable of asking myself. Please bring me a cappuccino now and I'll have a chicken and salad sandwich.'

She pushed past the crowded tables, and taking possession of the spare chair by standing behind it, said coldly, 'May I?'

Above the edge of the newspaper she saw only the suggestion of dark, wavy hair, heavy brows. He grunted something — not even a hint of encouragement in the sound, but she seriously needed a cup of coffee, so she ignored the hint and dropped into the chair.

In the cosiest, darkest little corner of the trendy coffee shop on the promenade of suburban Melbourne's bay frontage, she resigned herself to facing the newspaper propped in front of her by long, lean hands. Certainly not retired hands, she speculated idly, as she waited for her coffee to arrive, and no wedding ring.

Switching her attention to the newspaper, she scanned an article on a new Australian film, before transferring to a column which listed things to do today. Right now, she didn't want to do anything but indulge in a sea of indignation and search for ways to handle the precarious situation in which she'd become embroiled, back at the fitness centre where she worked. How dare Darren think he could get away with it?

Suddenly the top of the newspaper crackled and ever-so-slightly grazed her nose.

Startled, she cried, 'Excuse me?'

'Sorry.'

The paper lowered, blue eyes glanced up and acknowledged her presence.

'We're in what you might call a tight corner here,' a pleasant voice said.

He actually had a face! Quite an attractive one, too, in a roguish kind of way, Tessa observed. It was a contrast to the suave, good looks of Darren. The beast! She didn't want to think about him.

'Perhaps if people came in to eat instead of to read newspapers, it might ease the problem.'

Her voice reflected her irritation with men in general.

'I was filling in time, expecting company.'

He began folding the paper.

'Why didn't you say? I could have sat somewhere else.'

'I tried to.'

'You grunted. I took it as agreement for me to sit here. Besides, Angelo said it would be OK, and it's his coffee shop.'

'Having a bad day, are we?'

'No we are not. I am,' she replied icily.

'Now that's a coincidence. My day's not shaping up too well either.'

'Bully for you. It can't be as bad as mine, and you're adding to it.'

For comfort, she took a long drink of the coffee which Angelo had placed in front of her before dashing off without a word. A smile rearranged her companion's features. Lines crinkled around his eyes as he looked hurriedly down at his folded paper and drew a pencil from his business shirt pocket. Tessa guessed why he smiled so suddenly. She brushed the back of her hand across her lips to remove the cappuccino foam, before struggling to smile. He handed her a serviette, one brow raised. Her face hot, she patted at her mouth.

'Gone?'

He nodded.

'Didn't I tell you? I'm having a really bad day. Much worse than anything you could possibly match.'

His gazed fixed upon her as if he'd noticed her for the first time.

'How trickster draws a unit? Four words. Any ideas?'

She stared at him.

'What? How . . . who did . . . what?'

'Sorry. Thinking aloud. It's the cryptic crossword, and that's one of the clues. You should try cryptics some time. They're guaranteed to take your mind off your problems.'

He tapped the paper with his pencil, looked down at the small black and white grid, then his eyes lit.

'Got it. The answer is 'Pull a fast one'. Do you follow?'

He pencilled in the letters.

'Only people with a warped sense of humour do cryptic crosswords.'

'Better than no sense of humour.'

She tilted her head and strands of her long hair flicked across one cheek. She tucked the stray hair behind one ear.

'And they also have an irritating way of raising one brow.'

'Know a lot of people who do cryptics and raise one brow, do you?'

Put that way, it sounded ridiculous. She forced a smile. Why take out her bad mood on someone who happened along for no particular reason?

'Maybe not, but they all have this superior attitude,' she said sarcastically.

'I don't know why. Anyone can do cryptics and I'd be happy to teach you to raise one brow if you're interested in learning how to irritate people.'

He smiled widely.

'Thank you, but I'm sure I have enough irritating habits as it is.'

'OK. Since we're closeted together here, at least until you finish your coffee, let's play it safe and concentrate on the crossword. I'm referring to the puzzle, of course, not your contribution to this conversation.'

She patted her mouth with a serviette after taking another long drink, trying hard to convince herself his teasing manner amused her.

'Here's a clue a beginner like you

should be able to get. We're looking for a four-letter word for 'Don't eat so quickly.' Get it?'

Stupid of her, but she felt a hint of pressure to find the answer.

'No, I don't. And if you're trying to belittle me, forget it.'

'Come on. I reckon you're a bright woman. Think about each word separately and you'll put it together. It's not hard.'

She couldn't think clearly at the moment, not for anybody, including this man who searched her face for an answer she didn't have. He'd probably already dismissed her as bimbo. She would finish her coffee, forget the sandwiches, and find somewhere quiet, perhaps by the water, where she could decide her next move.

'I'm not in the mood for thinking. What I need is fresh air.'

She pushed back her chair. But to her alarm, he glanced at his watch and stood up.

'Me, too. Lisa's probably not coming

now. I'll join you.'

She heard his footsteps behind her. At the counter she forced money into the cashier's hand after he tried to pay for her coffee, and later when he pushed and held the door open for her, she swanned through it, her nose in the air. But out on the pavement, she realised she'd been petty. He meant well, and it seemed as if his girl hadn't shown up, so he'd had a disappointment, too.

'Thanks,' she said with little conviction. 'I hope your lady gets in touch.'

She began to stroll away, but oddly, her feet stalled. She didn't take horoscopes seriously, but at morning tea she always read them. Today, Leos were told they'd be placed under severe stress, but help would come from an unexpected source. My Cryptic Crossword could be the unexpected source from whom help might come.

Give yourself a break, don't start believing that nonsense, she told herself, and pushed off into the crowd of lunchtime diners and shoppers along the Esplanade.

Rick, her table companion, went into alert mode. His coffee acquaintance with the disdainful eyes was about to disappear in the crowd. He couldn't let her go, especially as he'd gone to so much trouble to arrange with Angelo for her to sit at his table. He caught up with her.

'You forgot your change.'

'Put it in the guide dog collection tin. It's not important.'

'Not as important as getting away from me, eh? I've been trying to think where I've seen you before.'

She eyed him with suspicion.

'I hope you're not trying to pick me up.'

'You can't blame a man for trying.'

He laughed, then snapped his thumb and index finger.

'Got it. The fitness centre. You work there, don't you?'

'Yes,' she said tight-lipped. 'I'm second in charge. I mean, I was.'

Alarmed he asked, 'You haven't resigned?'

His whole plan centred around her working there.

'I hope you haven't done something as foolish as walking out in anger. That's not very smart. You should think about it before you throw in a position you've worked hard to achieve.'

'I am thinking about it, and I don't need you counselling me.'

He'd hoped for an opening to discuss her position at the centre, her relationship to the manager, but after her icy response, he changed tack.

'Sorry, if that's what I seem to be doing, but hey, I'm grateful to you. You know, I've almost forgotten Lisa stood me up. Have you thought of the answer yet?'

They'd reached the steps down on to the foreshore picnic area.

'You mean as to why your day has improved and mine hasn't?'

He laughed.

'No, I was referring to the crossword

actually. You said you'd think better in the fresh air, and here it is.'

He demonstrated with his hands. Some people said his hands talked.

'It hasn't worked. I'm still in a lousy mood, and believe me in the hours left in the day, I plan to wallow in my misery. And here's some advice for you. You'd be smart to disappear, or you might feel the sting of my tongue. Men aren't my favourite people at the moment.'

Her cheeks glowed. She meant it. How to deal with it?

'Afraid I can't apologise for being a man, but if you don't mind me saying it, whoever this guy is, you're letting him get the better of you.'

'Only temporarily. He'll pay. I just haven't yet thought how.'

'Did he try something on?'

'You could say that.'

'OK. I get the message. You don't want to talk about it, but since we've both been badly let down, perhaps we could wallow in our misery together. I notice there's a picnic table free. I could go for some sandwiches and another coffee. I'm Rick Tremaine, by the way.'

'And I'm Mary Poppins. Good afternoon.'

She was sure mad about something, he realised.

'You can fly and sing, too, Miss Poppins?'

'Off the handle and off key. So beware.'

He probably wasn't meant to see her smile, but it encouraged him.

'It's far too pleasant a day to allow an unprincipled man to ruin it. Me? You're as safe as houses having lunch with me, with so many people around. We could finish the crossword together. It might help you focus afresh. If you're bored after that, promise, I'll zap out of here.'

She looked down at the steps leading to the grassy area beneath the pine trees. At least she was thinking about it.

'You're persistent, Mr Tremaine, and I could do with another coffee. OK, lunch, and that's it.'

'That wasn't so hard to decide, was it?'

She shrugged and followed as he led the way to the picnic table. Her sandals scrunched into the grassy knoll alongside him. He ventured a glance, saw a slight softening of her mouth. Was he making progress? She dropped lightly on to the bench seat.

'Fancy any particular filling in your sandwiches?' he asked.

'Ham's fine,' she said as if she didn't care.

'Not with pickles, I presume.'

Her eyes tilted upwards when she smiled. She was good-looking in a classy type of way, a bonus because he planned to spend lots of time with her in the next month or two!

'You're right. I've had enough pickles today. Make it salad, and a white coffee, thanks.'

Sitting on the bench, she tucked her hair behind one ear, and crossed her legs, as if resigned to spending time with him. He'd reached first base, and

14

so far it had been like picking his way through a sticky spider's web. He reminded himself it wasn't going to get any easier, if he aroused her suspicions.

'While I'm away you can think of the answer to the cryptic clue.'

She shrugged.

'It's not a satisfactory trade-off, but I'm Tessa Raymond.'

'Nice, Tessa. I'll get those sandwiches. Don't go away.'

He started to stroll off.

'You promised you'd give me a hint . . . er . . . Rick.'

She sounded vaguely irritated because he'd forgotten. A good sign. He'd engaged her interest.

'The clue's don't eat so quickly. Answer? A four-letter word which has something to do with McDonalds. I'll expect a solution when I get back.'

He grinned and strolled off, content that he was over the first hurdle.

On the edge of the bench, Tessa watched him make his way back to the coffee shop, her mind on his clue.

McDonalds — hamburgers, takeaway food? She smiled. She'd guessed it! Perhaps it meant she was at last thinking clearly and could tackle the problem with Darren maturely.

She eased back on to the bench, pleased with herself for the first time today. Childlike, she couldn't wait for his return to tell him she had the answer. And then she thought with a flicker of alarm, she hardly knew this man. Fifteen minutes ago they'd never met. Yet in that short space of time he knew her name, where she worked and she'd agreed to lunch with him. How on earth had it happened? Mostly because he'd been able to ease her anguish by diverting her attention, however fleetingly, to the insignificant. And, of course, his dark, attractive appearance hadn't done him any harm.

She tilted her head in exasperation. His looks had nothing whatever to do with it. He'd caught her at a vulnerable moment, challenged her with that stupid crossword. She glanced at her watch. He seemed to be gone an age. A knot tightened in her stomach. He wasn't coming back! He was probably in his office right now gloating to the blokes about the ill-tempered lady he'd met at the coffee shop, and how easily he'd talked her into lunch.

A typical man, she thought. If she could see his contemptible face one more time, she'd . . . What? Demonstrate how useful her fitness was? Useless probably, against a man built like Rick Tremaine. Around six feet, he was fit and lean. Her thoughts winged back to the gym, and anger towards Darren crowded her mind.

Thrusting her handbag over her shoulder, she jumped to her feet and strode across the grass. In the unlikely event that Tremaine did come back, he wouldn't find her waiting for him, no way. After she took a set of steps which led up to the Esplanade farther along, she merged into the crowd.

2

Tessa forced herself in the direction of Work Out, the health and fitness complex where she worked. She'd been impulsive in storming out earlier and saying she wouldn't be back. Rick Tremaine had done her a big favour by helping her to decide not to walk away from a position she'd worked hard to reach in a job she loved. Also, she had an aerobics session for young mothers this afternoon and she didn't want to let them down.

Now, she could see clearly that she'd played into her boss's hands by losing her cool and storming out. After his latest indiscretion, naturally he'd want to get rid of her, particularly as she'd threatened to go to his wife, whose father owned the complex. The alternative was to report him to the authorities. She pushed it to the back of her mind. She had the ability and the resolve to deter any further advances he made, and he knew it.

Besides, he was the one with much to lose if she exposed him — not to mention the media coverage he revelled in, and the accolades and business it brought the complex.

Anyway, she couldn't afford, financially, to walk away from her job. Having recently located a well-run and pleasant nursing home for her ailing mother, she'd committed to a loan to pay for it. Her position paid well and offered her flexible hours so she could occasionally spend daylight hours with her mother. You didn't give up those things without a fight because your boss thought his position entitled him to take privileges with you. Thankfully, Darren couldn't dismiss her without a great deal of fuss, because she had a year of her contract to run.

Sighing, she made her way to the aerobics exercise room. Megan, a trainee instructor, caught up with her.

'Tessa, Darren asked me to take over the afternoon sessions. He didn't think you'd be available for the rest of the day.'

'I expected to be delayed, but here I am,' she said brightly. 'Would you like to lead the class? It'll be good experience for you. I'll join the group in the back row so you can call on me for any help. I feel the need of a good work-out after the morning I've had.'

Megan beamed.

'Thanks. I'd love the chance.'

For the remainder of the day, Tessa dreaded bumping into Darren. It didn't happen. He knew she'd returned because she reported in at the front office, so she assumed he deliberately stayed out of her way, which suited her because she'd decided to wait until she'd had a good night's sleep before tackling him and hopefully coming to an arrangement which enabled her to keep her position and her dignity.

One solution was to rearrange their work schedules so they were rarely on duty at the same time. Another, the only really acceptable one, was that he change his ways and stop thinking of himself as God's gift to women.

In the indoor pool, the last training squad had finished for the night. Kane Fraser lagged behind and when everyone else had left, begged Tessa for the chance at a last attempt to improve his time for the fifty-metre butterfly. She smiled her agreement, encouraged by his enthusiasm. As he dived into the pool, she triggered the stopwatch. Without people, the huge area had suddenly grown disturbingly quiet. She shivered in a silence which made the smooth, splashing strokes of an accomplished swimmer resound eerily through the space and bounce off the high walls and ceilings.

She stiffened as a cool breeze disturbed the humid, chlorine-laden air. Behind her, someone had opened the door in from the darkened reception area and stood there, holding it open. She concentrated on Kane's figure in the pool, hardly daring to look. Surely it wasn't Darren, waiting to waylay her, waiting to tell her she was finished.

'What was my time, Tessa?' Kane called from the other end of the pool.

She jumped. Blast! The watching figure in the gloom had upset her concentration. She turned angrily, ready to pour scorn on whoever it was, but found to her surprise she could only make out the shape — a man, yes, maybe Darren. Maybe Rick Tremaine? Nonsense! She was being fanciful.

Kane reached her end of the pool, climbed out and claimed her attention.

'Come on, Tessa. What's my time?'

'Sorry,' she said. 'I goofed. It didn't register. Can we do it again tomorrow? I'm a bit weary tonight.'

He sauntered off, grumbling. Behind her a second rush of air swept in and she heard the door close. When she turned again, the unknown observer had disappeared. She shook herself and glanced up to the gymnasium area which overlooked the pool. A glimmer of light told her someone was up there. One of the maintenance men, she persuaded herself, and made a slightly nervous dash for the public changing-rooms. There she found the laughter among the female swimmers of the squad restored her equilibrium. Hot and sticky, she chatted as she waited in turn for a quick shower.

Later, at home, unsettled by the emptiness of the house without her mother, she searched for something to occupy her mind. Her glance fell on the newspaper. She folded it around the cryptic crossword, and looked for the clue, twenty-four across.

'Don't eat so quickly,' she read aloud.

A vague sense of achievement rippled through her as she wrote in the answer. Her only regret — she'd denied herself the pleasure of putting straight Mr Tremaine that she wasn't a blonde bimbo. Could she get a few more answers? But none of it made any sense, and she was too tired to push herself. She tossed it aside. Tomorrow she'd start getting the hang of them. If Rick Tremaine could do the wretched things, so could she!

First thing next morning Tessa went to the reception area and glanced through Darren's programme for the day, hoping to find an opportunity to talk to him. Unfortunately he had meetings scheduled until three o'clock. Shrugging, she asked Greg, the duty receptionist, to pencil in time for her in the afternoon, and then turned away. Behind her, she heard a voice she recognised, and swung round to find Rick Tremaine standing on the other side of the glass at the counter. Her heart fluttered briefly.

'Hello, again,' he said, as if he knew her well. 'Fancy running into you.'

Fancy, she thought cynically, especially as she'd told him where she worked. Had he come to ask why she scooted off yesterday? She stepped across to the counter and smiled at Greg.

'I'll handle Mr Tremaine's enquiry,'

she said. 'Would you like to take a five-minute break?'

'Thanks a bundle,' Greg said and pushed off.

She turned to the grinning Tremaine with an impatient shrug.

'How may I help you?'

'You persuaded me yesterday I should get fit.'

'I did no such thing.'

'Of course you did. You looked so good, I decided I could take a leaf out of your book.'

'Mr Tremaine, your compliment doesn't work with me. Besides, you look very fit.'

'Thank you. Now what sessions do you suggest I enrol in?'

Tessa sensed his insincerity. Why did he want to join a gym? She could think only that she attracted him. Flattering, but she wasn't in the mood for any man's advances, if that's what they were. She had a far more important problem to solve.

'None. You'd be wasting your time.'

As she spoke she heard the door behind her open. Thank goodness Greg had returned, but as she felt him draw closer, she cringed. The scent of Darren's after-shave invaded her nostrils.

'Tessa, you seem to be having some trouble. May I help here?'

As he stood beside her, she shook her head, furious, boiling to tell him where to go, but he ignored her and addressed Tremaine.

'Darren Connor, the manager. I understand from what you were saying you're interested in joining a class, sir. Weights, swimming, aerobics, power walking, a general workout? What did you have in mind . . . er?'

'Rick Tremaine, but I came in to talk it over with Tessa. We're acquaintances.'

She looked up surprised and felt Rick's eyes upon her.

Grateful he hadn't denounced her as unhelpful and testy, she said brightly, 'I'm dealing with it, Darren. We were about to sit down together and do an assessment.'

She had her pencil poised over the appointment book.

'Good. I'll leave it to you, Tessa. Good day, Rick. I hope you decide to come on board,' Darren said and moved away.

The door closed behind him.

'You're shaking,' Rick said.

'It's cold.'

'If you say so, but all I can see outside are blue skies.'

'It's draughty in here. Do you want to make an appointment or not?' she snapped.

'You suggested we sit down together. Why not? We could go out and sit in the sun. Get you warm.'

'Mr Tremaine, I have this uncomfortable feeling you're not really here to join a class.'

'I thought we'd progressed to first names,' he said with a grin.

She tilted her head to one side, exasperated.

'OK, Rick. But you haven't explained your real reason for being here.'

'At the risk of repeating myself and boring you, it's to get fit. Why else?'

She felt a surge of colour in her cheeks. He was teasing her.

'I wish I knew,' she said, disappointed at her lame reply.

'Call my bluff. Do an assessment. Then see if I take out a membership.'

Greg had returned. She put down her pencil, closed the book, and turned to him.

'Mr Tremaine and I will be discussing our various classes and memberships in the centre's coffee shop. Page me if you need me before my next session in fifteen minutes, please.'

She glanced at her watch and turned to Rick.

'Fifteen minutes maximum before my aerobics class. I think that should be ample time to deal with your membership.'

Lifting several leaflets from a stand, she vacated the reception area for the office exit and joined Rick. He appraised her intently, giving her the uncomfortable feeling that she was under-dressed, though the black tights and pink sleeveless top which hugged her body to just above her waist, were what you wore in exercise classes.

'Wait here,' she said and hurried to the staffroom to slip into an overblouse before rejoining him to go to the coffee shop.

She invited him to sit down while she went across and took up two polystyrene cups, popped in two tea bags and jetted boiling water from a stainless steel urn into the cups. Pushing the tea in front of him, she began her spiel, anxious to pin him down, push him into proving he was genuine about wanting to join.

'An open membership entitles you to the use of all our facilities. Cheaper passes are available to get you into one activity, such as swimming, aerobics, weight-lifting or self-defence,' she began.

'Why were you so nervous back at reception? Is Connor your boss?'

Tessa fought to compose herself. She certainly wasn't going to tell a stranger why her boss sent shivers of disgust up her spine. And yet, confiding in someone would have helped ease the shadows across her heart. Until her mother's stroke, she'd always been able to confide in her, and feel assured she'd receive sensible advice. Her relationship with Janet went beyond the mother and daughter bond. They were friends.

When a late teenager, her mother had been deserted by the man responsible for her pregnancy, and single-handed, she'd raised Tessa. Probably her severe stroke while still only in her forties had been helped along by her struggle to give her daughter a good and loving home life, values and a university education.

Tessa ran her finger along her cheek, tucking her hair behind one ear.

'Mr Tremaine, I was cold. I already explained why. May we get back to the type of membership you're seeking?'

'Suit yourself, but you're not fooling me. I think your boss was the man who made you so angry yesterday. If you talk about it, it might help.'

'I rejected your offers of a counselling service yesterday, remember? Why would I discuss my personal business with a man I hardly know?'

Her fingers gripped the pen she held.

'Because we're kindred spirits. Remember, I was let down yesterday, too.'

'And you're about to suggest we met by fate?'

'Well, it could be.'

'It was a chance encounter, Rick, nothing more. Can we get off the subject? Did you say what membership interests you?'

Rick decided to pull back. In his anxiety for answers, he'd pushed too hard. It would have been easier if she'd been less independent, and yet he found that quality in her admirable.

'I can't make up my mind. You say a full membership gives me access to all the facilities.'

'If that's what you want, but it's expensive, and you'll need a letter from your doctor giving the OK for you to participate in the more demanding activities.'

'Not a problem healthwise. I've recently had a full physical with the Hanover Foundation, and my company will pay for the membership. So, Tessa, where do I sign on the dotted line?'

She pushed a form across to him.

'You'll have to fill this in first. Return it when you have and we can go from there. Our physiotherapist will design a programme for you once you indicate your special interests. You mentioned your company.'

'Tremaine and Trus . . . '

He remembered in time he didn't want her to have the other name.

'Tremaine and Tremaine,' he corrected. 'My father was the original Tremaine. We're a small engineering company.'

'It's your company?' she asked.

'A family business,' he replied, looking down at the tea in the plastic cup.

Had she noticed his reticence? Would

it make her question even more his reason for being here?

'Drop the completed application form into the office next time you're passing, with your doctor's agreement,' she said, glancing at her watch.

'Now I must go. I have a class in two minutes.'

'Self defence?'

'Aerobics for women.'

'While I'm here, may I take a look around the centre? I'd like to get a feel for the various facilities.'

'Well,' she prevaricated before shrugging, 'it's not usual for nonmembers to wander around unescorted. Darren has a rule about that, but since you're intending to join . . . I do have your word on that, Rick?'

'Of course I'm joining. You have my word. Mind you,' he said grinning, 'I had your word you'd wait for me yesterday. It didn't help my ego to have two women desert me within the hour.'

'Sorry, but to be honest, I didn't think you intended to come back.'

'You don't trust men much, do you?'

'That's one thing you've got right. Must dash. See you later.'

'I don't suppose you thought of the answer to the cryptic crossword clue I gave you yesterday,' he called after her.

'I did. Tell you later.'

Tessa slipped away, and disappeared into a crowd of young mothers with strollers and cumbersome bags heading in the same direction as her. It reminded Rick of his mother, of the shopping expeditions with the pram, and how much she depended on him to help her with Sandon, who constantly occupied his thoughts.

The late, unexpected but much-heralded child of his mother's second marriage, Sandon's birth and childhood had sapped her energy. Rick, eight years his senior, became his mother's helper, and later, the spoiled child's protector. Not that he objected. He loved waylaying the bullies from the junior school on their way home and telling them to keep their hands off his little brother or else. It didn't take long for word to get around that Sandon should be given a wide berth.

Now, he could no longer protect his brother. It had all gone terribly wrong. He didn't think it possible, for he adored his gentle mother, but these days he was glad she wasn't here to know the truth. The memories hung heavy on his mind and impeded his progress as he made his way up the stairs to the gymnasium. He pounded his fist into the rail. Why hadn't he seen it coming?

A hand rested on his shoulder.

'Rick, old man,' the voice said, 'are you looking for the men's room?'

Darren Connor's tone held an edge of annoyance. The memories cleared from Rick's mind in a hurry.

'Connor,' he said in his friendliest tone. 'Tessa gave me permission to look around because I'm taking out full membership. That's OK with you, isn't it?'

'It's not usual without someone to

explain everything to you. Tessa should have arranged for you to be accompanied around the place. Women sometimes forget that the rules apply to them, too.'

He stood on a higher step, barring Rick's progress.

'She was rushing off to a class, but she talked me into full membership and in sponsoring several of my employees, so I guess she thought she could make an exception in my case. She's second in command, I understand.'

'Yes, she reports to me.'

Darren placed his index finger at the corner of his mouth as if thinking. Then he smiled and stood aside.

'A full membership and sponsorship, eh? You won't regret it. Of course you're free to inspect the gymnasium. No problems there. Why don't I take ten minutes and show you around myself?'

Rick groaned inwardly. So much for the hope that he could wander freely around the place, and he didn't like the way Darren Connor smiled.

Instinctively, he sensed something hidden behind the man's grin. Earlier he'd been convinced that Tessa felt an aversion towards her boss. It could be explained in terms as simple as that she was ambitious and he stood in her career path.

'I don't want to take up your time,' he said, hoping.

'Not a problem.'

Darren turned and led the way up the remainder of the stairs and into the large, well-equipped gymnasium. A catchy tune beat out, the various pieces of apparatus were in perpetual motion, the sweat dripping from the foreheads of the participants.

'You're free to use it any night but Tuesdays, provided you come before eight o'clock. We close the doors at nine-thirty. On Tuesdays, an élite group of swimmers has exclusive use of it.'

Rick nodded, looked around him, then adjusted his voice to be heard above the music.

'It's very well set up. I think I'll get

lots of use out of it. The door at the back, does that lead downstairs? It would be a quicker way up, wouldn't it?'

'It leads back to the basketball and netball courts, but we keep it locked. The teams who come for basketball and netball competition only pay a rental. If they had easy access to the gym they'd be up here like a shot helping themselves to free use of the equipment. I know that sounds tough, but ours is a privately-owned complex.'

'Don't give it another thought. I understand. I run a small business myself. Nothing as impressive as this, of course,' Rick said, working to get Darren on his side.

'I don't own this. It belongs to my father-in-law, but he gives me carte blanche to run it as I see fit.'

Rick laughed.

'Nice one,' he said.

'What?'

'As you see fit. Fit. I thought you intended the pun.'

'Of course I did.'

Connor's laugh lacked spontaneity, and Rick decided not to embarrass him further.

'So your father-in-law's only interested in the bottom line. Aren't they all?' he went on.

'You've got a close-fisted old so-and-so looking over your shoulder, too?' Darren responded.

This time his accompanying laugh sounded genuine. Rick nodded, confirming the lie. He owned his business, had no partners or shareholders.

'I can see we're going to get on like a house on fire.'

Connor's pager rang. He drew it from the back pocket of his shorts and spoke into it.

'Sorry, mate, I'm needed downstairs. Pop in for a drink after you've worked out one evening. I keep some of the hard stuff in my office for special thirsty clients.'

He tapped the side of his nose with his finger and grinned.

'I'll keep it in mind,' Rick replied.

He watched Darren leave, inspected one or two of the machines, and then strolled casually across to the door at the back of the gym.

'It's kept locked,' an instructor said, who must have followed him in soundless sneakers. 'You can't get back downstairs that way.'

Rick raised his brows.

'Yeah? I thought it might be quicker. I want to take a look at some of the facilities at the rear of the building.'

'Sorry, you'll have to go back the way you came. The boss keeps this part of the building private. He entertains influential clients in there.'

'I thought there'd be a staircase leading to the basketball courts.'

'There is. You joining the gym?' the man asked.

'Yeah.'

'Wanting to build up your muscles for that special little woman you fancy, eh? You've come to the right place.'

Rick thought of Tessa, but she wasn't

the reason he'd come to the fitness centre. She was no more than a means to an end. A knot of guilt in his stomach reminded him he hadn't expected to feel in any way uneasy about that. He'd set himself a strategy. He couldn't abandon it because he found Tessa Raymond distracting, appealing. He had to stick to his plan.

3

At exactly three o'clock, Tessa knocked on Darren's door and strode in without waiting for a response. He glanced up immediately and muttered, 'Come in. Sit down.'

The thought flashed into her head that he looked flushed in the face, but she dismissed it. Men like him were never embarrassed. She closed the door, using the time to tell herself to stay cool, to prepare for her next move. Crossing to his desk, she straightened her shoulders, jutted her chin, determined. He stood up, a familiar and often-used tactic he employed to demonstrate authority. She expected it and remained standing. Even so he looked down upon her, but not from a height which gave him too much of an advantage.

'Darren,' she launched into her

well-rehearsed piece, 'I hate to disappoint you, but I don't intend to resign. However, I do plan to take immediate action if you touch me again, or try to hinder my career.'

'Touch you? You make it sound like something sinister. It was no more than a friendly pat.'

'If I decided to, you know I'd have no trouble finding other women to back me in going to the sexual harassment board, not to mention your wife and father-in-law. I might even talk to the media.'

He paled visibly.

'You're over-reacting, Tessa. There's no need for that,' he blustered.

'You have a reputation as a womaniser around the corridors of this centre, so stop denying the obvious and listen. I plan to start a women's self-defence programme. First, for the female staff and later for clients. You will pay for an instructor to come in, and you will stay away from all classes where women are involved. This is your first and last

43

chance. Is that clear?'

Her stomach churned, her legs felt spongy, but she managed to sound resolute, immovable. He flopped on to the corner of his desk.

'Tessa,' he said, at his smarmy best, 'you're blowing this right out of proportion. OK, I admit it, I tried to kiss you. I was saying thank you for the wonderful work you do around the place. You're our best asset. I don't know what we'd do without you.'

'You won't have to. You and I both know you're lying. I'll look around for a self-defence instructor, advertise the classes, and present you with regular reports. Good afternoon, Darren.'

One step at a time, she told her wobbly legs, as she covered the space to the door and tugged it open. Outside, she paused for several deep breaths, and then walked away. She needed a coffee.

Though he found it hard to curb his eagerness to push on with his plan, Rick had decided it was prudent not to return to the centre for a few days. Then he felt sharp, ready to make some progress and made for the gym. Consulting the white board which listed the sessions in progress, he noted Tessa was on duty in the aerobics room. Wandering down the hallway towards the room, he found himself jigging to the fast beat of the music before he reached his destination. Even if the music hadn't led him there, the frenetic shouting would have.

'Come on, left, left, up, up, and stretch, and stretch. Wow! Come on, use those muscles. Across, across, push and push. Wow! Keep it going.'

He wouldn't have thought it possible for Tessa to pitch her voice to that range, but it was unmistakably hers. At the door he glanced in. Watching her stretch and bend he saw what he'd failed to appreciate earlier. It had already registered that she had an eyebrow-raising body, fit and shapely. Now he observed how supple, how disciplined it was as it acted effortlessly, gracefully, to her commands.

He'd gone in that direction hoping to 'accidentally' meet up with her when she finished, not to gape. Now he moved on. If Connor or one of his muscled instructors noticed him hanging around the aerobics room during a female session, it wouldn't reflect well on his chances of gaining membership. Checking his watch, he wandered farther down the corridor expecting her to finish any time. He heard the music slow down, Tessa's voice soften. Warm down, he thought with relief.

The women began to stream along the passage, chatting in groups. He hurried ahead of them, uneasy lest they misinterpret his presence. But as they crowded the narrow corridor he realised he could have been invisible. Their minds were on other things like a shower, their performance, children to collect from the crèche, shopping.

A straggler, red-faced, breathy, passed by.

'I was hoping to talk to your

instructor. Has she left?' he asked.

'She usually tidies up the room after the session. She'll come by shortly.'

'Thanks,' he said, and walked confidently back towards the exercise room, though to be honest, he felt a touch apprehensive.

Suppose she turned down his offer of lunch. Where did he go from there? Gaining her friendship was his best chance of getting the information he sought. He found her lugging a pile of mats across to the corner when he put his head around the door.

'Hello, again,' he said.

She paused and a mat slipped from her grasp. He hurried across to retrieve it, and then relieved her of the rest of them.

'Where do you store these?' he asked, congratulating himself on the fortuitous timing of his arrival.

'In the corner,' she said, wiping her brow. 'Now this is one rescue attempt I welcome.'

'My speciality, always being in the

right place at the right time.'

She reached for a towel from the back of a chair and mopped the sweat from her forehead.

'Thirsty work.'

She smiled, and he grabbed the opening.

'May I take you for a drink? Coffee?'

She shook her head.

'Sorry. I've got some paper work to deal with. Are you here for a workout? I haven't noticed your application for membership being processed.'

'That's why I came.'

He pulled an envelope from the pocket of his cotton shirt.

'You don't have to give it to me personally.'

'When we parted, you said you'd see me later.'

'I meant later as in weeks, months, maybe never.'

'I suspect you're stalling because you don't have the answer to that cryptic clue, and here was I hoping you were ready to move on to today's puzzle over lunch at Angelo's.'

When Rick Tremaine grinned, things seemed to turn sunny. Tessa had noticed it before. But a man needed more than an appealing grin and persistence to influence her. Still, her mind argued, lunch at Angelo's had a certain attraction. Spending lunch breaks in the staff-room fielding jests from the male weight trainers about her new self-defence programme was starting to bore her. Time away from the centre would be a refreshing break from the familiar day-to-day routine, and set her up for a staff meeting scheduled for this afternoon. These days she felt tense when she had to mix it with Darren around the boardroom table. Her heart did a quick flip-flop at the thought, but she managed a light reply.

'Of course I've worked out the answer. It doesn't take a rocket scientist,' she said.

'And, it is?'

She sensed he didn't quite believe her

and decided she enjoyed prolonging his uncertainty.

'All in good time. We'll talk about it over lunch.'

'You mean you're saying yes?'

He seemed genuinely surprised as she consulted her watch.

'I'll see you at Angelo's in an hour, and this time I want a front row table.'

She tossed her towel in his direction and hurried away before she thought better of her decision.

'At your service, ma'am. I'll also have the cryptic folded, ready for us to attack. Bring your pen,' she heard him say, and smiled to herself.

Rick couldn't believe the ease with which she'd agreed. Maybe in some contradictory way they'd connected, and then he reminded himself that before he started thinking about her as a woman, he had to know he could trust her, had to know more about her and the authority she carried within the centre. On the face of it, Tessa seemed involved mainly with the day-to-day maintenance and running of the exercise sessions, but until he had more information, because she was second in charge, he couldn't dismiss the idea that she knew everything that went on in the business.

Until he confirmed the extent of her influence at the fitness centre, she remained on his list of people to be investigated. In fact, he decided, no staff member could be eliminated from his list of suspects.

As he made his way across to the Esplanade, a welcome sea breeze cooled him down. But still he questioned his chances of finishing the task he'd started. He'd started out with no more than an idea, no detailed plan. It wasn't the way he normally operated. In making contact with Tessa, he'd thought arrogantly that as a woman she'd be an easy target. Now he questioned that judgement. What if he discovered she was involved? Would he be ruthless enough to make her pay?

Pushing his doubts aside, he found a

table at the front of Angelo's bistro, folded the newspaper around the crossword section, gazed out on the passing parade, and watched out for Tessa. The sun glinted on the glass, creating shadowed patterns across the table. During summer the beachfront shops took on a festive air. It was hard not to feel the vibes. He promised himself when it was all over he'd start enjoying this trendy, energetic bayside town again. But for now, he had to remain alert, cautious.

Tessa appeared on the pavement outside and, for some odd reason, the crowd seemed to fade into the background. She stood out as she moved with effortless grace in her thigh-length white shorts, a colourful, sleeveless top and dark sandals. He noticed, too, how her hair still glistened with dampness when she flicked it back from one side of her face, a mannerism she used a lot. Could be it signalled nervousness at lunching with him, and why not? They hardly knew one another, had nothing in common, not even their methods of keeping fit. He preferred swimming in the sea every morning to visiting a designer gym. He felt a bit tense himself at the prospect of lunching with her, short-changing her, cheating on her.

He stood up and waved as she entered. She responded with a half-smile and made her way across to the table.

'Best seats in the house, I see. Do you have some influence with Angelo?' she asked.

Her comment made him uncomfortable.

'I'm working on it.'

Sitting down, she again tucked strands of hair behind one ear.

'Angelo said you're a regular. Strange I haven't seen you here before.'

'We probably come at different times. I'm not normally here for lunch.'

He diverted the conversation.

'You see, I have the cryptic crossword ready, but let's eat first.'

He handed her the menu.

'What'll you have?'

She took it, but studied him.

'So what brought you in here last week?'

He raised his brows.

'Could be I was hoping I'd get lucky and meet a pretty lady.'

She coloured slightly. He hoped he hadn't overdone it.

'And she didn't show up,' she said as her gaze fell to the menu.

'I don't follow.'

'Lisa, your lunch date. She stood you up. Have you forgotten already?'

Tessa sensed an uncertainty in his flippancy.

'Lisa made a habit of standing me up.'

She wondered why a woman would do that. He wasn't handsome exactly but occasionally his smile upset the rhythm of her heartbeat, and she enjoyed the badinage they'd shared. Pointless to deny it.

'You don't look like the type of man

who let's people stand him up.'

'Not as of last week. Lisa's in the past. Now, I've decided to order a bowl of noodles. What about you? A drink first?'

She discerned an anxiety to get off the subject of Lisa. Why?

'An open salad sandwich on rye, thanks. And yes to the drink.'

'Angelo's on his way over, and Lisa's out of the picture. Did you sort out your problem of last week? Did you deal with your boss?'

Just when she'd relaxed he had to mention Darren!

'All sorted,' she replied rather curtly.

'You don't sound too sure. When he came into the reception area last week, I could almost feel your shiver of disgust.'

'It really doesn't concern you. I'm a big girl. I can look after myself.'

She laughed mockingly.

'Sure, but I could see how just being near that guy upset you.'

Tessa shifted in her chair, uncomfortably warm as he gazed intently at her.

She could deny what he'd said, or be up front and tell him her story. In truth, talking over the situation with someone she trusted might ease the uncertainty and confusion she felt over the course she'd followed to deal with Darren. But Rick would probably advise her to seek legal advice; to sue her boss and the fitness centre for sexual harassment. She tried to hide her shudder at the thought. Even if she won the case she'd be dragged through a court hearing, receive unwanted publicity, and probably be ostracised by some potential male employers. She'd be the loser.

Besides, as a prospective client, and a virtual stranger, Rick wasn't the person to confide in. Suppose he bumped into Darren at the centre, felt the need to say something to him or, horror of horrors, agree with her boss that she'd been oversensitive and imagined he'd tried to kiss her. She hid her shaky hands in her lap, curved her lips.

'I agree with you. He's smooth to the point of oiliness, but he can be charming. That's what pulls in the clients, especially the women. I might as well tell you I was mad at him last week, but it had nothing to do with his ego. I don't like other people countermanding my decisions, especially males who object to reporting to a woman. There's a fair bit of that going on. The gym is staffed primarily by men who seem to think muscles equate with brains and authority. But I've sorted the problem. I let it get the better of me briefly and stormed out. I have you to thank for reminding me I was wrong. You persuaded me to return.'

'Any time.'

'I can't believe I ignored the three golden rules for women in business.'

'And they are?'

Before she replied, the noodles arrived. He picked up a fork.

'Looks good. I don't know about you, but I'm famished.'

'Me, too,' she said, forking up some noodles, starting to relax.

'Hey, you didn't tell me your business rules.'

'It's women's secret business.'

'I could pass it on to my female staff if it has merit.'

'I hope they don't need it, but for what it's worth, I try to live by it. Don't be negative, don't be aggressive and don't be emotional. My mother handed it on to me, and it's always worked in the past. Mum used to be a senior administrator in an international photographic company.'

Though she said it with pride, her voice fell away when the image of her mother today slipped into her mind.

'So she's retired now, and you're carrying on the family tradition as a senior administrator in a major health and fitness centre?'

He was making conversation, trying to sound interested. Tessa guessed that. Perhaps he was even flattering her because he thought that's what she expected. Why would he care about her mother or her career?

'Yes, to both questions,' she replied evasively.

His follow-up question surprised her.

'I know you're second in charge at the centre but what does that involve, apart from the sessions you take? Who runs the business side of things? It has to be a multi-million dollar venture and I can't believe Darren . . . '

He gestured with the hands she'd observed so closely last week, the fingers which wore no wedding band. He dropped them to the table as if to pass judgement on Darren Connor's ability to spearhead a business of that dimension. It had occurred to her from time to time that Darren didn't have the ability to control a successful enterprise, and yet he had the figures on the bottom line. She smiled.

'I hope you're not planning a take-over?' she said to Rick with a smile.

He laughed.

'Just supposing, what would I be up against? Who are the major shareholders?

Where and when do I make my first raid?'

'Darren's father-in-law, Joe Cotchin, owns two-thirds of a chain of health and fitness centres, but Work Out is the most successful. That's why my boss is the golden-haired boy, and why his daddy-in-law rewards him handsomely. Sorry, but you don't stand a chance of budging the shareholders. They're happy with the spoils their investment gives them. What's your real interest anyway?'

'I'm a business man. Naturally I have a broad interest in notably successful companies.'

'Ah.' She smiled. 'Now I understand why you're joining up. You want to observe some of our methods from inside. Remember, I suggested at the start you didn't need a fitness régime, but if I were you I wouldn't go poking my nose behind closed doors. Darren's sensitive about that kind of thing.'

Rick's shoulders tensed. Had he asked one question too many and too soon, made her uneasy? His laugh sounded a shade too generous.

'You haven't seen my swimming or you wouldn't say that.'

'You swim? Where?'

'In the bay, early mornings when I can.'

He forced himself not to raise a brow. She'd already said it irritated her. He tried again for a definitive answer by watering down his earlier question.

'You didn't tell me what you do at the centre, apart from the women's aerobics sessions, of course.'

'Actually, I joined the centre as an accountant with an interest in the fitness market. These days I look after most of the day-to-day finances and purchases. We have accountants to handle the big stuff. That, thank goodness, leaves me free to devote time to the fitness side of things. I really didn't think I'd get so wrapped up in the sessions and the people. I love it.'

Oh, no, Rick thought. If Tessa was an accountant, she'd recognise any irregularities in the centre's financial reports.

That had to mean she could be implicated. He had to get over this feeling that he didn't want her involved. He had to stop thinking about her as a woman.

She was smiling.

'What's so amusing?' he asked, brushing a finger across his bottom lip, surmising he had a piece of noodle sticking to it.

'The other side,' she said, amusement sparkling in her eyes.

He ran his tongue over his bottom lip. 'Gone?'

'What a big mouth you have, Mr Wolf,' she said with a giggle.

Her words had a strange effect upon him. He felt hot, uneasy, but found the wit to retort.

'All the better to eat with!'

Her eyes shone as she studied him. He patted his mouth with the napkin.

'I hope you're not going to sit there and watch me tuck into the rest of the meal.'

'You do it like this,' she said, twirling

her fork into the noodles and efficiently lifting them to her mouth.

Enticing lips, he almost said before placing the last of his bread roll into his mouth to stall any temptation to tell her she was upping his temperature.

'More coffee? A pastry?' he asked.

'It sounds nice, but I should get back. I have a two o'clock session and then a management meeting.'

Her voice again lost some of its sparkle which had him speculating that the meeting wasn't something she looked forward to. If only he could convince her to confide in him. Give it time, he warned himself. You've come a long way in seven days. There's no real hurry. He wasn't going anywhere, and then he reminded himself that he couldn't get on with the rest of his life until he knew the truth about Work Out.

Tessa stood up.

'Thanks for lunch. I enjoyed it. I owe you now for two things.'

He stood with her, pushed her chair in.

'I don't follow.'

'Last week, you, a stranger, advised me not to walk out on my job. It pulled me up with a jolt, prompted me to think with my head instead of acting on impulse. If I hadn't gone back to the complex that afternoon, I'd have played into the hands of certain people.'

'You owe me nothing. It's been my pleasure. I reckon it must be tough for a woman being in charge of a gym with all that male ego around.'

'I'm up to it.'

She smiled, though in truth, after the episode with Darren, she hadn't stopped questioning her ability to deal effectively with sexist males in the workplace. Shaking off her uncertainty, she went on.

'Perhaps we can do lunch again? Next time, I pick up the tab.'

Tessa wasn't at all sure why she suggested the idea. Clearly she'd again acted emotionally, but this time not in anger, but with a feeling of, could it be expectation? She tossed away the idea.

She felt nothing more than pleasure in his company, even when he challenged her.

'I've got wall-to-wall lunch time meetings for the next few weeks.'

Disappointed, she strolled ahead of him to the till. Was he declining in a polite way? Assume it, she persuaded herself, pretend nonchalance. You're dealing with enough at the moment. Say casually you'll see him around at the centre, and walk away. When she reached the receptionist, she turned to say exactly that, but he spoke first.

'Would you have dinner with me one evening, Tessa?'

She smiled. It was so unexpected, so pleasing. And why? It had something to do with his laid-back manner and his dark, roguish looks. But really, the fact that last week she'd met him at exactly the moment when she needed advice from a level-headed person had an air of unreality about it, as if it were not a chance encounter, but a preordained meeting.

Rick Tremaine had appeared in her life so unexpectedly and at an incredibly troubling moment in her life, she wondered vaguely at its significance. She admitted silently he intrigued her. She wanted to know more about him. Dinner would be a starting point.

'Thank you,' she said. 'I'd like that.'

'Formal or casual? The Regency or Lygon Street? Your call.'

She glanced at the clock on the wall and gasped.

'Where has the hour gone? I'm sorry about this, Rick, but I must run. Give me a call or ask for me when you come to the gym next time.'

'What about at home?'

She slipped a business card from her purse and handed it to him.

'I work such odd hours, wherever,' she said before hurrying to the door.

The last thing she wanted was to give Darren cause to criticise her, but as she strode along the pavement, a glance at her watch told her she'd panicked unnecessarily. She had ten minutes to get back to the complex which was only one block away from the Esplanade. And then she remembered she hadn't given Rick the answer to the cryptic clue.

Silly really, but she needed him to know she'd worked it out. Turning quickly, she hurried back to the coffee shop. She pushed open the door, looked around, but he wasn't there. Angelo was at the cappuccino machine.

'I suppose Rick's left?' she asked.

He grinned.

'So pleased to see you two hit it off real well, eh? I wipe the sweat off my forehead. I worry I could be doing the wrong thing.'

'The wrong thing? I don't understand.'

'Mr Tremaine, he say to me to put you at his table last week. He want to meet you.'

'Excuse me? He asked you to put me at his table?'

'But it OK, eh? I see you like him.'

'No, Angelo, it isn't OK,' she said quietly.

Then she swung on her heel and left.

4

Rick didn't understand it. On his visits to the gym he received almost VIP treatment in the weights' room, but any time he enquired about Tessa, there was always a negative response. Either she wasn't in, or wasn't available. Why was she avoiding him?

Finally he knocked on Darren Connor's office door.

'Come in, old man,' the manager said in his smooth manner. 'How can I help you? No problems with my staff, I hope.'

'No,' he said. 'I've been trying to catch up with Tessa. I guess I'm coming in at the wrong times. I've left messages, but she doesn't respond. I wondered if there's some rule here at the centre which precludes her from seeing members out of hours.'

Darren moved to the front of his desk

and propped on the corner.

'We don't encourage it, but, well, we can't stop nature taking its course. But you'll find our Tessa's an odd girl. Good at her job, mind you, but let's be honest here, she's one of these new-age women. Aggressively protective of her sex, hates men with any authority, and imagines they're all lusting after her. On more than one occasion she's threatened legal action. I mean, she's attractive, but not what you'd call irresistible, especially when you get to know her well. How well do you know her, by the way?'

Well enough, Rick thought, to realise either Connor was blind, or he had a grudge against her. He pocketed hands which longed to hit out at the supercilious Connor.

'I hasten to assure you, I'm not interested in her romantically. I'm surprised you keep her on if she causes such unrest among the staff,' he said, hoping the hostility he felt wasn't reflected in his tone.

'You're in business, old man. You know how sensitive these issues are. I mean, the slightest thing and they're off to legal aid, or trying to get up a class action. It's a pain. I'm biding my time with her. She's on a contract which runs until next winter. After that . . .'

He allowed the sentence to hang in the air.

'So you can't help me?' Rick asked.

'I'm wondering why you need to talk to her. Can anyone else help?'

'I promised I'd lend her a tape. She's been trying to buy it for ages,' he lied glibly.

'Leave it at the front desk. We'll pass it on. Don't forget if you're ever working out after six, drop in when you've finished, for that drink.'

'What about tonight? I'm off to the gym now. We can talk fuller on new-age women. That is, as long as your office isn't bugged.'

He heard Connor's laugh as he departed, and hated himself for making such a sleazy statement, but his secret agenda demanded behaviour normally repugnant to him. Now he had something else to do which disturbed him as much. Tessa had given him her business card which listed her home number and the centre's. If he could find out where she lived . . .

Greg was on duty at the desk.

'I'm waiting for Tessa,' Rick said.

'She already left.'

'Oh, no! I promised her I'd catch up with her. I've got tickets for a big concert tonight.'

'Wow. Lucky her,' Greg said.

Rick shrugged, took out his mobile phone and her business card, pretending to dial her number, and spoke in Greg's hearing.

'Tessa, yeah, I managed to get the tickets. Sorry about the mix-up in times. Sure I'll bring them around on my way home.'

Then he ended the call.

'Blast! I forget to get her address. Can you believe that?' he exclaimed.

'She's not far from here,' Greg

71

obliged. 'Milton Street, number four.'

A spontaneous smirk of satisfaction almost gave him away.

'Thanks, mate. The next free tickets I get are yours.'

Rick sauntered off to the gym, wondering how long it took to become good at this kind of subterfuge and whether, at some stage, it ceased to trouble you. He was sick to death of pumping iron and pacing the treadmill, sick to death of men with bulging muscles and egos to match, but the thought of his brother kept him at it. He was playing a game, perhaps a dangerous game, but one which only he could play.

Rick glanced at his watch. Six thirty. The place had grown gloomy and quiet. In the changing-rooms he showered and tugged on clean shorts, a T-shirt and joggers before making his way to Connor's office. He had no idea what he hoped to achieve by the visit, but he might get lucky. As he approached the office, he heard voices from within and considered barging in or eavesdropping by the door. Too risky, he decided, and knocked.

'Yes?' Connor replied, sounding imperious, impatient.

'It's Rick Tremaine.'

'Come in.'

Rick knew the young instructor who stood on the other side of Connor's desk by sight. He was big enough, muscled enough to take care of himself, yet at this moment Rick sensed his discomfort, his domination by the manager. Perhaps it was the wariness in the young man's eyes as he surveyed Rick or was Rick allowing his contempt for Connor to cloud his judgement? He warned himself to tread carefully lest his feelings about the man became obvious.

'You've got your orders, Jack?' Connor demanded of his instructor, who grunted, 'Gotcha,' as he turned to leave.

Facing Rick, Connor said, 'Good timing. We were just winding up our discussion about a new piece of equipment. Good of you to drop by. I was about to call it a day but I'm in need of a drink.'

Rick observed Connor tidy his desk, put a number of files and what looked like a cashbook into a drawer, lock it and shut down the computer.

'Still keep paper records?' he asked as casually as he could.

'Petty cash stuff mostly.'

'In my business there are occasions when I need a hard copy.'

'Sure, that's right. I don't recall you saying what business you're in.'

'Engineering, civil. We design and build bridges, roads, buildings. Had a hand in this complex, as a matter of fact.'

He glanced around the room.

'Reckon it could do with some updating.'

'Touting for work, are you?'

'Only observing. We've got more than we can handle now. We recently lost one of our most talented designers.'

'Tough. The best always move on, chasing the big dollars, eh? Let's get out of here.'

Rick fingered away beads of sweat from his upper lip. His brother, Sandon, hadn't been chasing big dollars. He'd been chasing dreams.

Connor retrieved his jacket from a stand, swung it over his shoulder and, plucking a bunch of keys from his belt, strolled to the door. Surprised that the drinks weren't in Connor's office, alert, Rick spoke casually as they moved into the passageway.

'Are we going somewhere special?'

'They say every man needs a shed. Mine's a bit upmarket, but it serves the same purpose,' Connor answered.

'Yeah? Where a man can do what a man has to do?'

Connor laughed.

'Couldn't have put it better myself.'

Rick suppressed alarm at how easily he'd mouthed such a crass reply, and joined Connor in laughter, as he followed him through the almost empty gym. Ah, he thought, simmering with impatience, when they arrived at the locked door he'd noticed on his first visit, I'm about to find out what's behind it. Connor swiped a key card through the lock before turning to him.

'I don't think I mentioned that nobody, but nobody, gets in here without my say-so.'

'You old fox! What're you keeping behind closed doors? You don't have to worry about me, mate. I reckon I've been around long enough to know you and me have a taste for good wine and . . . er . . . women.'

The door swung open. They entered a quite large, tastefully-furnished apartment. Connor may be a sleaze bag, but one with expensive tastes.

'What's your tipple, Rick?' he asked, crossing to the bar.

'Whisky, with ice. I'm still sweating after a spell in the sauna.'

A long glass of mineral water would have gone down well, but he had to keep playing the macho man with more than an eye for women if he were to get closer to Connor and his operations.

'Nice little set-up,' he commented as he accepted the drink.

'Cheers,' Connor said, and swallowed his drink in one gulp. 'So what do you think of my shed?'

'Every guy's dream, eh? Sleep here sometimes, do you?'

'Only when my wife's out of town. Another drink?'

'Sure, but I need the bathroom first.'

Connor indicated with his arm as he poured himself another drink.

The bathroom was large, equipped with shower, toilet and double basins and a wall of mirrored cabinets. Rick flushed the remainder of the whisky down the toilet, filled the glass with water and drank thirstily, refreshing his dry mouth. Next he chanced a look into one of the cabinets. Toothpaste, brushes, shaving gear, lotions, after-shave, painkillers — nothing unusual. But then he'd given Connor warning of his visit. He had to get out of here.

He accepted another drink, tried to look relaxed as he reclined in a large, leather chair, and chatted about business, the new tax system, anything but women, thank goodness.

Finally Connor asked him with narrowed, questioning, eyes, 'So what's your real interest in Tessa?'

'She's a good-looking girl.'

'And you're having trouble winning her?'

'You could say that, but I don't accept no for an answer easily.'

Connor stood up, glancing at his watch.

'Well, old man, don't say I didn't warn you. She's into feminism in a big way. Good luck! You're going to need it.'

Rick rose, too, thankful that he'd brought things to a close.

'Reckon I am, but I like a challenge.'

Connor slapped him on the back.

'Mate, if only you knew.'

'You leaving now?' Rick asked.

'No. I've got a few prospective clients to see first.'

Hadn't Connor said earlier he was about to call it a day?

'Up here?' Rick asked casually.

'Sure. They're corporates. I like to impress them.'

He led the way to the door, anxious, Rick sensed, to get rid of him.

'Keep up the weights. If you're not making satisfactory progress, let me know. I might be able to suggest another course of action.'

Rick heard the door lock as he closed it behind him, and breathed easily for the first time in half an hour. He'd learned nothing that he could use, but having been inside the room, next time he'd know the layout, have a plan, and Connor wouldn't know he was coming.

Upstairs, the gym was noisy, with people coming in for evening workouts. Pumping iron had never appealed to him. He'd never understood Sandon's interest, though he'd encouraged him because it undeniably made him a stronger, faster distance swimmer, a possible Olympian.

Rick showered at home, changed into casual trousers, a polo sweater, and headed for number four Milton Street. How would Tessa react when she discovered he'd got her address by a form of trickery? Should he tell her or let her find out for herself? Why had she refused to take his calls anyway? Suppose she'd discovered his real reason for joining the centre? His stomach clenched. Surely he hadn't been that careless.

Four Milton Street was a small but engaging semi-detached, single-storeyed brick house with dark green lace woodwork edging the roof of the veranda, a neat garden and hexagonal tiles on the pathway and veranda's surface. In the gloom of descending evening, a slit of light escaped from a long gap between the blinds and the casement window. Someone was home. He pressed the brass button on the solid door, his fingers mentally crossed.

No sound of feet inside, no sound of anything. Frustrated, he gave the button a second solid stab, but restless after what felt like long, fruitless minutes, he turned away with a feeling of uselessness. A car pulled up in the street as he left the veranda for the path to the fence. The void in his stomach was replaced by feelings of expectancy, of relief. Tessa climbed from the car, locked it, and finally looked up to find him opening her front gate for her.

He stood aside, gestured her to pass, playing it cool.

'At your service, madame.'

She tossed her head, passed him by, then turned.

'What are you doing here? I thought you'd have received the message by now. I don't wish to see you ever again.'

'Don't you think you owe me an explanation? I mean, I did help you save your job, and I did help you out when your boss ... You thanked me, remember?'

She raised her shoulders.

'I'm really not up to this, but you'd better come in before my neighbours see what's going on.'

'Nosy, are they?'

'Supportive. They know I'm on my own.'

That really got to him. Some of the stuff Connor had said about her reactions to men flashed into his head, stuff he didn't, couldn't believe.

'You don't think I'd harm you? Tessa, you can't think that?'

'Not physically, no, but you're here, aren't you? Invading my doorstep when you know I don't want to see you. Take it from me, you showing up is all I need tonight to really push me to the limit.'

He could see the tension in her eyes, in the tightness of her usually lithe, free-flowing movements. But something told him to linger, a sense that her hostility towards him was a veil she'd cast over something much more distressing.

'May I?' he asked softly, hoping she'd hand over the key, but she brushed him aside, pushed the key into the lock, twisted it with a jerky movement and pushed open the door.

'Now,' she pronounced, 'don't expect to get comfortable. First, I will tell you why this will be our last meeting and then you go quietly.'

'Of course I'll go if that's what you really want. Haven't I always been true to my word?'

The heels of her shoes echoed as she strode down the passageway as far as the first room, where a light already burned. She turned into the doorway, waited for him, her dark eyes flashing. He took a long breath. What irked her and how on earth could he ever retrieve the situation between them with any credibility?

Suddenly his heart told him he had to, told him what had started out on his part as a self-serving attempt to build a relationship with her had crash landed. She no longer represented a means to an end. She turned his feelings upside down, confused, yet electrified him, signalled possibilities.

Facing him, her eyes accused.

'True to your word? How dare you! You've lied to me on at least one occasion. For instance, Lisa. There is no Lisa, is there?'

He groaned. She'd found out he'd engineered their first meeting. Best to be open and admit there had never been a Lisa. Tessa Raymond wasn't a woman to be sweet-talked or jollied along.

'Sure, I made her up. Look, I'm sorry, but I wanted to . . . '

'I'm not interested in what you want. I am interested in knowing your real reason for joining the fitness centre. I'm forced to ask myself what else you've made up to get friendly with me? Damn it, Rick, I thought you were different. Are all men Connor-types? I actually liked you. I liked your openness and your honesty. Honesty! Huh. More fool me. I thought we could be friends.'

With a cynical laugh, she collapsed into a chair. The light caught her eyes. They glistened with tears. He felt so guilty, wanted to hold her, to comfort her, to tell her the truth. But he held back. He'd already made too many mistakes. Standing awkwardly, his legs apart, he displayed his hands.

'We can be friends. I'd like nothing better. OK, I admit I asked Angelo to sit you at my table that day. I'd seen you around, wanted to meet you.'

Tessa dabbed at her eyes with a tissue and shook her head.

'Forget it. Not tonight. This really isn't the time. I'm not up to this.'

'What's really troubling you? I don't believe you're crying because I liked you enough to set up a meeting with you.'

'I'm not crying,' she said, trying to hold back the tears.

'They look suspiciously like tears to me, Tessa. And if you feel like crying, you go for it.'

He moved closer, challenged her resistance, her earlier irritation towards him. He looked so strong, so dependable, so real on a night when nothing else did. She edged forward and sat down on the settee.

'Your timing is bad, Rick. I've just arrived back from the nursing home. Earlier I had word that . . . that my mother was . . . was dying. When I arrived there, I was too late. I didn't even get a chance to say goodbye to her. She wasn't just my mother, she was my best friend. It isn't fair. It's all so unreal. I want to wake up and find it hasn't happened.'

He sat down beside her.

'Would a hug be in order?'

She nodded.

5

Tessa felt his arms circle around her. She slipped her arms under his. His body felt warm as his hand softly massaged her back as she rested her head against his chest. In this moment of accepting, her strength ebbed from her taut body, the tears she'd worked so hard to contain throughout her mother's illness came in an outpouring of grief. The chill in her heart slowly thawed.

'I'm . . . I'm sorry,' she managed as the sobs subsided.

'Go for it,' he said quietly. 'Cry all you want.'

And somehow it didn't matter that he'd misled her, because at this moment he understood how she felt. She stayed in his arms, silent, for minutes, long enough to regain her strength.

'Never take your mother for granted, Rick. I hope you see her often. Tell her you care,' she said.

'She died a few years back, Tessa. She was a very special person.'

He meant it. She heard sincerity in his voice, in the gentleness of the tone, the slightly faltering words.

'You obviously loved her, and I'm sure she knew it. What happened?'

Tessa released her arms. He let her go, and wiping the remnants of tears from her face, she slid back into the cushions.

'Pneumonia. She was always fragile. She had my brother when she was in her early forties, and adored him, but his birth left her weak, and she didn't really recover her strength. When her husband died in a road accident, well, it didn't help. She was only forty-eight when she died.'

'I'm so sorry. Both our mothers were much too young to die.'

She shook her head. Saying the words was far easier than believing them. Her thoughts ran on.

'Mum was seventeen when she had me. Her partner refused to take responsibility, so she left her home town and raised me alone.'

'She must have been a remarkable woman. You said earlier she had a senior position.'

'She educated herself, worked her way up through her firm, but she insisted I go to university, get a degree. After a struggle with boredom as a financial adviser, I found the job at the centre, and discovered the fitness industry was where I wanted to be. After that we were game enough to take a bank mortgage and buy this place.'

She leaned against the arm rest with a sigh.

'It was going so well for us until . . . until a few weeks ago when all our dreams came tumbling around us. She suffered a severe stroke.'

Tears misted her eyes again. She dabbed at them, pulled herself up from the settee, afraid, even shy, lest she edge back into his arms.

'Why don't I make us a cup of tea?'

He stood beside her, placing his hands on her shoulders.

'You sit down. I'll make the tea.'

'You don't know where everything is.'

'I'll find it. You're looking at a practical guy, here.'

'I'll come, too. I need the company.'

'Lead on, Macduff.'

She appreciated his attempts to cheer her up, but couldn't manage a smile, not yet.

Tessa loved the efficient, little kitchen she and her mother had had remodelled to open into a compact dining area. They'd achieved a feeling of space using double glass doors which led on to a paved section suitable for outdoor entertaining. The kitchen light illuminated the outside patio. It looked and felt empty without her mother, triggering memories of the hours they'd spent together on balmy evenings, talking, planning, laughing.

'When you marry . . . ' her mother often said.

'If I marry,' she'd replied, always unable to imagine a future without her mother.

'When you marry and move on, this little house will be ideal for me to grow old in.'

Tessa felt a lump in her throat. She picked up the kettle and filled it at the sink, hiding her grief, lest Rick's sympathy cut through her restraint and bring on a second flow of tears. Though she wasn't a person who cried easily, genuine sympathy always touched her, and her heart told her his concern was unquestionable. He removed the kettle from her, plugged it in and pressed the button.

'I thought I was doing this.'

'I need something to do.'

'You know where the cups are, don't you?'

She reached for two mugs from an overhead cupboard, heard him say, 'I like your set-up here. It's neat, comfortably informal.'

'It works for us.'

Then she remembered there was no longer an us. A mug slipped from her grasp and shattered on the floor. Rick kneeled beside her, took her hands.

'Let me,' he said, and, offering no resistance, she allowed herself to be led to a chair and sat down.

She watched him pick up the pieces, wishing she could as easily pick up the pieces of her shattered day, and dispose of them in the waste bin.

The kettle shrilled its boiling message before clicking off. Rick rinsed his hands at the sink and turned to her.

'Tessa, tea isn't what you need right now. Do you have any brandy?'

She nodded, her lips curved gently in agreement, but the satin eyes had lost their sparkle.

'In the cupboard above your head.'

Finding it, Rick located a couple of glasses and half-filled one with the amber liquid. He handed it to her before allocating himself a smaller amount, remembering that tonight he'd already downed a few mouthfuls of whisky. But this drink, he needed. Tessa's grief reminded him, painfully, of his own loss. It reminded him of why he'd staged the meeting with her, and the melancholy which came over him had a large slice of guilt attached.

A sensible guy would get away now, before he said things he'd regret, things such as he wanted to hold her again, to smell the sweetness of her, feel the touch of her lips against his mouth. He swallowed the brandy in one shot. It caught in his throat as he made up his mind.

'Are you going to be all right?' he asked. 'Can I call anyone for you?'

'I'm fine. If I need anyone, Meg is next door. She'll come in.'

'I'll leave my mobile number. Ring any time. If you need help with the funeral arrangements, I've had some experience.'

'I'll be fine,' she repeated. 'Thanks for the hug, too. It helped.'

'Would you like me to come to the funeral?'

'It's up to you.'

'Can I call anyone to let them know?'

'If you're going to the centre tomorrow you could leave a note for Bill McCormack. He has the cleaning contract and is a special friend.'

'Right. Bill McCormack, in charge of cleaning, you said?'

'Tell him the funeral arrangements will be in the paper.'

'Will do. I hate leaving you. Perhaps a neighbour . . .'

'I'll be fine.'

He kissed her softly on the cheek, and stepped away before temptation to hold her again challenged his common-sense.

'Good-night,' he muttered.

As he closed her front door, he felt lousy about leaving her, and yet he knew the value of being alone for a brief period after the death of a loved one. Grieving could be very personal. Still, he knocked on the front door of the adjoining house, spoke to the woman, Meg, an older, quietly comfortable person, whose distress at the news of her neighbour's death was quickly set aside out of concern for Tessa. She agreed to pop in in half an hour or so and spend the night if that's what Tessa wanted.

Rick's journey home was desolate. He had his conscience to deal with. He could no longer keep the truth from Tessa. As soon as possible he'd explain what had brought him to the centre and how it involved her. He would confide in her, ask for her help.

Tessa woke to find Meg standing beside her with a tea-tray. Her eyelids felt unresponsive as she opened them. She'd slept briefly, but heavily, dreamless. Her nightmare started now.

She smiled her thanks. Meg pressed her to ring Rick, who had told Meg he'd offered to help Tessa with the arrangements.

'A woman needs a man around at these times,' Meg comforted.

'I've done very nicely for the last twenty-four years without one,' Tessa said lamely, but throughout the trauma of a day which had to be organised, she found herself remembering his arms about her and the almost peaceful strength she drew from that brief interlude.

With everything finalised for the funeral, Tessa pressed Meg to go home at around five o'clock. She promised to ring her later. Alone, she picked up the phone and tapped in Rick's number. She left a message about the date and time of the funeral and hung up.

★ ★ ★

Rick had dashed off a note to Bill McCormack and was pleased to find Greg on duty at the reception desk when he called into the centre.

'You heard about Tessa's Mum?' Greg asked.

'Yes. Tough, eh? Will you see Bill

McCormack gets this note as soon as possible?'

'You can give it to him yourself. He's giving the changing-rooms a quick spit and polish in preparation for the school swimming carnival this afternoon.'

Until this moment it hadn't occurred to Rick that as the head cleaner, McCormack would have keys to every door in the complex. Could he be trusted? Could he be persuaded to give him access to Darren Connor's shed. His earlier visit there had whet his appetite. It had a feel about it that urged Rick to return, alone and unannounced.

Could McCormack make that possible?

He found the older man mopping the floor in the changing-room for the disabled. When Rick called his name, he stopped, leaning on his mop.

'What can I do for you, laddie?'

Rick grinned. Laddie? A leap of the imagination!

'I'm a friend of Tessa's. Bad news I'm

afraid. She specially asked me to tell you her mother died yesterday. The funeral arrangements will be in today's papers.'

Bill took a handkerchief from the pocket of his overalls.

Was it the heat or did he have tears in his eyes? Rick liked him instinctively.

'Marvellous, gutsy woman, Janet Raymond,' he said. 'But she wouldn't have wanted to go on the way she was. Couldn't talk, totally dependent. I reckon it's for the best.'

Rick agreed before looking about him to make certain no-one was around. Holding a finger to his lips, he indicated silence to McCormack.

'Mr McCormack, this probably isn't the best time, but I might never get another opportunity, so I'm going to bite the bullet. Tessa tells me she's confided in you that Connor's been pestering her.'

'She has.'

He sounded cautious. If only Rick could get McCormack on his side. He picked his way carefully through the words which crowded his mind.

'She's a great lady, and I think it's time people knew exactly what kind of bully-boy her boss is.'

'You like her, eh?'

'What red-blooded male wouldn't?'

'So what're you planning to do? How do I fit into your plans?' he said in a friendlier tone.

How much dare he tell McCormack? Rick skated around the facts.

'The other night, Connor invited me up to his private rooms for a drink.'

'I hope you're not going to take up too much of my time to reach the point. I have to get this job finished, or I'll be out of a job.'

Only then did Rick realise he'd allowed his passion for finding out the truth to affect his judgment. If he involved McCormack and the man lost his contract, he'd have another thing on his conscience.

'Forget it. I'll give my idea some more thought.'

Rick turned to leave. McCormack resumed his task, but as Rick reached the door, he spoke quietly.

'I reckon you're talking to me because you want to get into the so-called shed belonging to Connor. You reckon something fishy's going on up there, don't you?'

Rick swung around, adrenalin pumping his heart.

'Spot on. I'd like time alone up there to have a quiet look around.'

'And then what?'

'It might be better if you don't know. Nothing dodgy, but I don't want you to get into any trouble.'

'It's all conjecture, anyway. I can't help. I don't have a key to the inner sanctum. My cleaning jobs are done by appointment with the boss's henchmen, and when I'm in there cleaning, one of his muscle men hangs around. You know what I think?'

'Tell me, Mr McCormack.'

'Bill, call me Bill, eh? I think there's something illegal going on, with women, maybe. I don't wanna know, mate, unless, of course, Connor upsets our Tessa again. I'd risk my job for her any time.'

'Good for you. Look, Bill, I think it might be better if you forget our little chat. Better if Tessa doesn't know we've been talking about her. She's a very independent woman. Besides, I'd hate to be responsible for you losing your job. But thanks anyway.'

'No worries. You get back to me, laddie, if you're worried about our girl. Reckon I could find a way into those rooms if push came to shove.'

Rick left, unable to decide whether he felt disappointed or positive.

★ ★ ★

When Tessa hadn't heard from Rick, she redialled his number.

'I need company. I don't suppose you could come over?'

He sounded pleased.

'Give me an hour to finish up here

101

and I'll be knocking on your door. Would you like to dine out, or shall I bring a takeaway?'

'Let's decide later. Food doesn't really appeal at the moment.'

'That's understandable.'

He made no fuss about her eating or not looking after herself. He understood. She realised it was one of the qualities she admired most in him. She'd conditioned herself not to expect that of men, but Rick was different, in so many ways.

After changing into a clean white T-shirt and shorts, as she brushed her hair she thought she felt her mother's presence, heard her say an oft-repeated phrase.

'Always try to look your best, Tessa, no matter how you feel or what the circumstances.'

Her imagination was working overtime, of course, but it influenced her to pinch a little colour into her pale cheeks and apply a light touch of lipstick.

It didn't make sense, but nothing had

since she received the news of her mother's death. All she knew was that for once in her life, she'd stopped being sensible. She would never have cried in the arms of a practical stranger, a man for goodness' sake, before yesterday. She would never have waited, her heart suspended, her emotions totally confused, for a man to knock on her door, before yesterday. She didn't believe in the supernatural but she felt an odd kind of reassurance. Their meeting hadn't been a chance encounter as it happened, but could it have been destined?

Fanciful, if you like, but she felt a quiet reassurance, as if her mother were nodding her approval. She left the front door open and suddenly he was beside her. His thumb caressed hair away from her forehead, his lips touching it lightly. How natural it felt, how soothing to have him supporting her, showing he cared.

'You OK?' he asked, stepping away.

'Getting there.'

'Want to talk?'

'Maybe, maybe not. I don't want to be a cry baby again tonight. I kind of think I'm all out of tears, anyway.'

He lifted her chin.

'Crying is good for the soul. You go for it if you want.'

'I've made a pot of tea.'

She led the way to the kitchen.

'Did you cry when your mother died?' she asked.

'Not physically, no. I had to stay strong for my younger brother. She adored him, spoiled him. He was devastated when she died, poor bloke.'

They sat at the small, round table. She poured the tea.

'I'm sure she loved you, too,' she said, her voice soft.

'Yes, but she didn't love me the way she did my brother. It didn't worry me. You see, the difference is, she disliked my father, and I guess I inherited some of his traits, particularly his determination. He was much older than her and neglected us shamefully for his business interests. After he died of a heart attack, she married a man she idolised and together they had my brother. I think I mentioned earlier, her pregnancy was unexpected. She couldn't believe it when her son arrived safely, perfect.'

'You didn't mention his name.'

She folded her fingers around her cup, sipped from it, gazed at him over its rim.

When he replied shortly, 'Sandon,' she sensed uncertainty in the way he turned his eyes away.

'It's an unusual name.'

'My mother's maiden name.'

'Where's your brother these days?' she dared to ask.

Rick had come prepared to tell her everything tonight, but now, somehow, the reminder of Sandon and his mother persuaded him to wait.

'He's not around any more.'

'Oh? You must miss him. I'd like to have had a brother, but it wasn't meant. Do you ever wonder about fate? I mean, about how and why things happen.'

He gestured with open hands.

'Yeah, I do, like us meeting. I know it had nothing to do with chance, but maybe fate played a part.'

Tessa's eyes looked startled.

'How strange. I was thinking that before you arrived.'

'It's natural. We have a lot in common, and I've grown to . . . er . . . grown fond . . . damn it, I care a great deal about you, Tessa.'

He engaged her attention, caught her glance. Her dark eyes glistened.

Tessa tried to look away, to avoid giving voice to what was happening between them, to convince herself it was the natural response of someone who already felt the pain of missing her mother, but his searching gaze refused to release her. She stumbled over her reply.

'Rick, I . . . I can't. I mean this is an emotional time for me. I don't want to . . . I mean I can't.'

'Understood. I'm not asking for a commitment. I spoke out of turn.'

Oh, no, Rick thought, clattering his cup back into its saucer. What a hamfisted jerk I've been. It's too soon after losing her mother.

In the silence which followed, he heard the glass door slide open. She had moved out into the shadows, silhouetted against the evening light, the gold rim of the china cup in her hand glinting. He thought, an empty, lonely feeling gripping his heart, what if she disappears, becomes part of the darkness itself? I could lose her without ever really knowing her. He raised his voice to reassure himself she was still there.

'Tessa, I'll join you.'

She didn't reply. He found her slumped in the chair outside.

'I didn't mean to upset you. You OK?'

She placed her cup on the garden table.

'You didn't upset me. I guess I'm still

a bit fragile. You know, Mum and I used to sit out here and talk for hours on evenings such as this.'

'Talk all you like. I'm a good listener. By the way, is everything OK now, about that stunt I pulled in arranging to meet you?'

'I suppose I should have been flattered, but after Connor, I don't trust the male species easily.'

He sat down on the opposite chair.

'He made — how can I put it delicately — unwanted advances, didn't he? That's why you were so mad that first day I met you.'

'You guessed it, and of course you were right.'

The moonlight caught the gloss of her lips. He thought she smiled gently, and suspected she found it easier in the darkness to open up to him.

'Feel better now you've shared it with someone?'

'I did tell someone else.'

He felt vaguely disappointed. Was there another man in her life?

'You surprise me. I thought I was your confidante.'

'Sometimes I surprise myself. Bill's an old friend. I mentioned him earlier. Remember? He has the cleaning contract at the centre. I took him on after he lost the contract at my mother's firm. She recommended him and he hasn't let me down. He's been a good friend during Mum's illness. He promised to keep a lookout, observe Connor's movements.'

'But he's not going to be much help. Cleaners are only there when everyone has gone. So what else have you done to clip Connor's wings?'

'I talked to him.'

'Tessa, the man's an egotistical cretin. Talking won't help. Lies, deception, they're a way of life for a guy like that.'

'I didn't have much choice. If I'd gone to the owners they wouldn't believe their son-in-law was a nasty piece of work. It would have been my word against his. But I warned him if he touched me again or I found out he'd been making unwanted overtures to other women in the centre again, I'd be knocking on the door of his house, talking to his wife.'

'And his response?'

'He scowled and said Stephanie was too smart to believe my lies, and he'd already told her about me constantly flaunting my body at him. I feel nauseous every time I think about it.'

He tilted her chin with his finger.

'I hate you being there. Can't you find another position?'

He dropped his finger as she stuck out her determined chin.

'Cut and run? No way. I've put in the hard graft at Work Out. I refuse to be forced out by a creep. It would suit him if I disappeared, but I plan to stick around and keep him honest with the other women.'

She sounded fiercely independent.

'He won't step out of line again. I insisted he fund a self-defence course for female staff which will soon be offered to the public. I think I've got him on the defensive. He looked like a trapped rabbit when I mentioned I'd go to the media. Bad Press would kill the centre, and he knows it.'

'I haven't had much to do with the guy, but there's something about him. My mother would have said something about his eyes. I wouldn't trust a man-eating shark with him. And I'm not just talking about his womanising. He likes money and what it buys. I doubt if his back would ache no matter how low he stooped to make a fast dollar.'

Rick sensed her shift in the chair, the lifting of her shoulders.

'But he already had a life of luxury. He married money, and he's turned the health and fitness centre into gold. Work Out was struggling for a few years, but when he came on board, he turned it around in a year.'

'How, I wonder. What's his secret?'

His eyes had grown accustomed to the moonlight. He saw her shrug.

'Who knows? Part of it has to be his suave manner, his good looks. But let's not talk about him. It pollutes the air.'

'Before we close the subject, I'm reminding you if you ever need help, I'm only as far as a phone call away.'

'Why should you care?'

'I'd love a reason to punch the creep. But it's more than that. You and I, Tessa, we connected right from the start. You feel it, too, don't you, the bond between us?'

Tessa did feel it, more and more, and it seeded hope in her heart for the future. Did it have something to do with the loss of mothers who'd meant so much to them? Or a mutual recognition that Darren Connor was a prize fool? Their independent natures? A similar sense of the ridiculous? Those things added up to them being kindred spirits.

But their relationship went further, deeper. It had blossomed quicker than a bud develops into a full-blown rose and had a quiet beauty about it. She would like to have articulated her feelings better, but the words failed her.

'I think I know what you mean,' was all she said.

6

Rick stayed on the edge of the funeral service lest he appear an intruder. He hadn't known Janet Raymond but respected her for the high regard in which her daughter held her, and the outpouring of affection from the large number of people who gathered in the chapel to say farewell to her.

As they began to disperse, he moved forward to say something comforting to Tessa, but paused when he heard his name. Swinging around, he saw the fresh-faced kid he knew as Kane.

'You're Sandon's brother,' Kane said. 'You used to drop him off at the pool. Remember me? Kane Fraser?'

'Sure, I remember. You trained with Sandon. What brings you out here today?'

'All Tessa's squad came. Dad had me transferred to her team after Sandon got into trouble. I told my dad Sandy, as we called him, wasn't a cheat, but he said he was a bit old for me to be knocking around with. Anyway, Tessa's an ace coach. But I stay in touch with Woodsy's mob. He was good with us blokes, and he gets us together for a bit of a barbecue now and again. It makes the long hours of training worthwhile.'

Rick always felt empty, desolate when he thought of his brother. He asked a question which, until now, he'd always thought he knew the answer.

'Did Sandon ever complain to you about the time he put in at the pool, Kane?'

'A bit. We all have those downers when we ask ourselves why we're doing it. He used to say he looked up to his big brother and wanted to prove to him he could do something really worth-while.'

The teenager brushed hair from his forehead and his face went crimson.

'It's warm inside with so many people, isn't it?'

Rick guessed Kane's flushed cheeks resulted more from embarrassment, for the lad had given away one of Sandon's secrets. And, damn it, he was the one who should have felt embarrassed. Instead, he felt deep remorse. A sensitive man would have realised he was pushing too hard, driving his kid brother to feel a need to earn his esteem and approval. But, no, Rick had honestly believed if Sandon succeeded as a national swimmer, it would make him more responsible, improve his accountability, give his mother the joy and satisfaction of seeing her younger son succeed.

Ambition for Sandon had blurred his vision! He'd played a major rôle in what had happened to his brother. That's partly why he'd become obsessed with finding the truth.

He shrugged.

'He was over the moon when he got into the Australian finals. We all were,' Rick said.

'The fellas in the squad, too. And

then, when he dropped out, we wondered . . . I miss him. He was always larking about. He knew how to have a good time.'

The lad paused there.

'I feel awful, you know. I wanted to go to his funeral, honest I did, but Dad came down pretty heavy on the idea.'

His eyes sparkled with moisture.

'Don't distress yourself, Kane. I know how it is with parents, and usually they're right,' Rick said kindly.

'It was so sudden. Dad said he died from a heart attack.'

Rick nodded.

'Yeah, that was the coroner's finding. He put it down to a heavy training régime, which . . . '

Rick caught a familiar fragrance and turned to face Tessa. A tear stain had patterned a path through the light make-up on her cheeks, but her dark eyes managed a smile which stirred his heart.

'Tessa,' he began.

'Two of my favourite men,' she said

gently. 'Thank you both for coming.'

'I was real sorry about your mum, Tessa. Are you gonna take a week or two off?' the young lad asked awkwardly.

'Thank you, Kane. I'll be back in a few days. Now, excuse me, I must move on, speak to more people.'

'May I drop by soon?' Rick asked.

'Give me a couple of days, Rick.'

He nodded.

'If there's anything I can do now . . . '

'I'll speak to you later.'

Tessa was caught up by a couple of people wanting to express their condolences and wandered off with them. Rick touched Kane's arm.

'Stay out of trouble, young fella,' he said, before striding from the chapel to his car, a man weighed down by guilt and regrets.

How much had Tessa heard of the conversation? Did it matter? When he saw her next, he would tell her anyway what had brought him to the fitness centre. Until now he'd dealt in half-truths because he didn't know the facts, and because he still felt he needed to make excuses for his brother. But Tessa would understand. He already felt easier in his mind.

★ ★ ★

Tessa sighed. It was two days after the funeral, and still sleep eluded her. Exhausted, she dropped on to the bed, plumped up the pillows and closed her eyes. Having ridden an emotional roller-coaster for days, spent her tears, she yearned for a long, dreamless sleep, but it didn't happen.

Her thoughts kept circulating back to Rick. She thought they'd reached the stage where they could share everything, yet she'd had to find out by chance of his young brother's death, when she overheard his conversation with young Kane. Trying to recall Rick's words to explain to her his brother's absence, she remembered the phrase he used.

'He's not around these days.'

She took it to mean Sandon had moved on, left the area, but now a shaft of disappointment lanced through her, for Rick had let her go on believing that. Perhaps because of his grief? Perhaps because of her interest in fitness and the manner of the young man's death?

She wrinkled her nose. None of those explanations satisfied her. Surely a young man entering a demanding training routine would have had a physical beforehand. Wherever he trained, she thought, they'd been slack.

Her thoughts leaped to her fitness centre, to the hushed discussions behind raised hands as she'd entered one of the management meetings a while back. When she asked for an explanation Darren mentioned Brett Woods' distress. He'd just heard that one of his young squad had died suddenly at home, of heart failure. She remembered the pall of gloom which settled over Brett, his moodiness, but it lasted only as long as it took for him to report that the coroner declared the centre in no way to blame for the lad's death.

Her mind worked overtime now. She held her breath and asked herself, could that boy have been Rick's brother? It would have to be a remarkable coincidence, but coincidences did happen. If only she could remember the boy's name. Perhaps she had never known it. She shook herself. Had it been Rick's brother, he'd have told her. She pushed the idea to the back of her mind, and recalled the management team's discussions about rethinking their policy on young people joining their squads.

After the young man's death, they'd decided, with litigation so common these days, to update their procedures to cover any possibility of being sued. But after the inquest, all the talk had come to nothing. She should remind Connor to put it back on the agenda.

The voices in her head circled back to Rick. She yearned to see him, to feel the warm intimacy of being with him. And yet, until she could dispel these new, unwelcome doubts from her mind, she wouldn't feel free to continue her relationship with him.

She picked up the phone, dialled the centre and asked for Brett Woods. She had to know the name of the young swimmer attached to her centre who had died so tragically . . .

Rick had been speaking to Tessa on the phone every day to reassure himself she was OK. Today he tapped out her number as arranged. They were to have dinner. The call switched over to the answering machine. Where was she? She knew he was to ring. An uneasy feeling settled in his stomach.

He was sure she'd heard his conversation with Kane Fraser at the funeral, and he'd expected her to make a comment about it, but she hadn't. Was she upset that he let her go on believing Sandon had left town? His relentless search for the truth about Sandon had been turned on its ear by his growing love for Tessa. He'd met the right woman, but at the wrong place and at the wrong time.

He put his mobile into his trouser pocket, picked up his car keys and slammed the door of his office. As he did so, it hit him that, without noticing, and without his mother to remind him, he'd developed the self-destructive traits of his father. He'd made his business the cornerstone of his life, and the only person he truly trusted was himself.

On the short journey to Tessa's house, his heart beat with an eagerness to arrive, to hold her, to tell her he'd fallen in love for the first time, but cautioned himself to tread slowly, to assess her reactions first. Yet, when he swung open the gate of her house and strode up the short path to the veranda, with a rush of impatience he called her name, once, twice. But that, and pressing the doorbell drew no response.

Where was she?

The door on to the back patio stood open. As he charged inside he called her name again, and this time he heard sounds coming from the top of the house. He arrived at the bedroom door to find her yawning as she sat up, her dark eyes clouded with sleep, her hair appealingly mussed up.

'Rick, you're here,' she said, sounding surprised, rubbing her eyes. 'I've had a wonderful sleep, at long last.'

'Sleeping Beauty, and here I was out of my mind worrying about you. Thank goodness you're safe.'

He sat on the bed, cradling her in his arms.

'When you didn't answer your phone, when you didn't answer the door, I thought . . . '

She placed her arms about his neck and drew him close.

'Thank you for caring. I'm glad you're here. The doctor gave me a pill to help me sleep.'

Tessa swung her feet to the floor.

'I can't believe how hungry I feel,' she said in surprise.

Relieved, he smiled.

'Would you like to go out for a meal?'

'Not tonight. I'd prefer to stay in. Help me put some pasta and a salad together and we can talk.'

'You're on,' he said.

She nodded, slipped her feet into sandals, ran her hand through her hair, and brushed down her trousers.

'Will I pass?'

'With flying colours. It's good to see you smiling again.'

'You have that effect on me.'

He put his arm about her waist and they walked to the kitchen.

As they prepared the meal and began to eat, she spoke of the simple funeral service, of the people who'd supported her with their messages, of old friends she hadn't seen in years. But for Rick it was the prelude to a difficult, but necessary conversation, a conversation he could no longer put off. He finally opened the subject.

'There's something I need to get out of the way before we can move on. I owe you an explanation, Tessa.'

She smiled gently. The deep sleep had eased her mind. She'd begun to think more clearly.

'About your brother? I didn't mean to overhear your conversation with Kane, but it has raised some questions. I was distressed to hear Sandon had died, but it disappoints me that you didn't feel you could tell me.'

He put down his fork, eased back in his chair.

He's uncomfortable, she thought, and urged him, 'You obviously had your reasons, but whatever they are, I'd be privileged if you could share them with me.'

'I didn't tell you because, in a way, I've involved you.'

She suspected that, but decided to wait for him to go on.

'There's a chance you may have known him. He swam in Brett Woods' squad.'

'You're talking about Sandon Truscott, aren't you? I made some enquiries once I knew you'd lost your brother. It took me a while to make the connection, because I'd forgotten you mentioned you had different fathers.'

'You could have asked me,' he said quietly.

'But would you have told me the truth, I mean the whole truth?'

'Yes. I had my reasons for keeping quiet, but now I want to tell you everything.'

When Tessa saw the uncertainty in his eyes, sensed the tension in his body, she touched his hand.

'What happened, Rick? Tell me.'

He leaned back in the chair.

'Sandon was a distance swimmer, fast over eight hundred metres, and he loved winning. He had so much potential, but when he didn't touch first in the titles last year, I discovered later he went shopping for help. And he found it.'

'Rick,' she said quietly, 'what do you mean he went shopping for help?'

127

'Drugs. What else? He started experimenting. It seems some of the other kids knew, but I was too busy with my business to notice, too busy feeling proud of his achievements. I screwed up big time.'

'You can't blame yourself. He wasn't a kid.'

'Of course he was a kid, spoiled by his mother, indulged by a big brother. He didn't have a chance to grow up.'

'No more talk of blaming yourself. It's the dealers out there who are to blame.'

'Tessa, I've never unloaded on anyone like this before. I was blind, blind to the fact that I kept pushing him. I used to try to psych him up to win for his mother, tell him how proud she'd be if she were in the stands watching.'

He shook his head.

'Yet I knew he was easily led, prone to temptations, had been all his short life. I kept telling myself if he made the Australian squad it would build his

confidence, make him more responsible. When I look back . . . '

The anger and pain in his deep blue
eyes stirred her very being, but she
judged that by talking now, he might
have a chance to work through it.

'You're being too tough on yourself.
You weren't his keeper.'

'In a way I was. I promised my
mother I'd look out for him. Thank
goodness she wasn't around when I
confronted him, asked the big question.
He admitted it and promised to stay
clean.'

'He didn't keep his promise?'

Without answering, he left the table
and paced across to the patio doors.
She lost his face, but could feel the
tension, see his taut shoulders outlined
against the evening light as she waited
for his answer. But he remained silent,
staring out into the gloom. Should she
prompt him?

'Rick, the autopsy said he died of
heart failure. If drugs killed him, why
didn't the coroner pick it up, give it

some publicity, try to get to the source? Why blame the training?'

He swung back to face her.

'I asked myself that over and over. I wasn't satisfied with that finding, so I spent hours on the internet, and on reading. I've talked to sports medicine doctors and national coaches. I know I've got the answer, but until I can prove it . . . '

He shrugged, made a futile gesture with his hands. Tessa took a long breath.

'What did you find out?'

'For quite some time, twenty otherwise fit and healthy males are believed to have died from taking a drug which enhances the oxygen-carrying capacity of the blood in the body. I believe Sandon's death adds to that statistic. Oh, I need air.'

He opened the door and strolled out. Tessa followed quickly, afraid he might leave, afraid he might have said his last word. She found him slumped in one of the chairs.

'Sorry, Tessa, you can do without this. I didn't mean to get so hung up.'

'Talk to me, Rick. Don't clam up now. I need to know more. For example, how do you reconcile your opinions with the coroner's finding?'

'Sandon didn't show any signs of a heart problem. He was strong, healthy. The effects of this latest blood-doping scam can last up to three weeks, but current testing methods only detect its presence for a maximum of three days. It's the only explanation for my brother's sudden death. I think the drug was in his body for days before he died, in which case it wouldn't show up in the post-mortem.'

He sat forward in his chair.

'It's been my mission these last few months to nail the culprits, to put a stop to their little game. I reckon I know who they are.'

Tessa eased forward, her heart racing. She thought she knew what he was about to say. She thought she knew what their so-called chance encounter in the coffee shop was all about, and it had nothing to do with Rick finding her attractive. Had he used her, exploited her? Did he genuinely care for her, or did he see her as a means to an end? She had to know.

'You know them?' she said, uncertain, anxious.

'Tessa, you're not going to like some of this, but it has to be said. I believe Sandon was supplied with drugs at Work Out.'

A sick feeling settled in her stomach. She wanted to lash out, to defend, to be unconditionally protective towards the centre, and yet, Rick wouldn't make the claim if he didn't have something on which to base it.

'I can't believe this. It's nonsense. You actually think someone at the centre is involved in selling drugs?'

'Not someone. I think there's a team of dealers working out of the place.'

'Go on,' she said softly, her voice weak. 'What proof do you have?'

'Nothing that the law will listen to.

I've talked to the police about my suspicions. They told me to come back when I've got something substantial to report. That's why I've been hanging around the place, trying to get some idea of what's going on around there.'

'And you lied when you said you engineered our meeting because you found me attractive, didn't you? You planned to use me. And that's exactly what you've been doing. I think you might even suspect me of being involved. Care to explain yourself, Rick?'

7

Rick stood up, pocketed his hands, took a long breath as he looked down at her, wishing like the devil he could deny her accusations.

'This is so hard for me because you're right. In the beginning I targeted you, but that soon changed once I met you, got to know you. And sure, it occurred to me you could be involved. After all, you're second in charge. I don't feel proud of it, Tessa, but I know now how wrong I was.'

'And I'm supposed to say thank you because now you trust me, I suppose.'

'Tessa, I know I've hurt you. Can you ever forgive me? After I met you, got to know you, well, I fell for you in a big way. I planned to tell you many times, but then you lost your mother. I didn't want to lay it on you then.'

'Excuses, Rick. If you really fell for

me, as you say, you'd have told me days ago.'

Rick ached at the sadness, the disappointment in her voice.

'I'm asking you to understand that my determination to get to the bottom of Sandon's death has been at the top of my agenda for months. I hadn't thought of anything else until you came along and threw me into a spin.'

His appeal touched Tessa immediately. She'd been petty, self-centred. Her fragility, her sensitivity to Rick's misrepresentation of himself mattered little when compared to the main scenario, the astonishing charge he'd made against the fitness centre.

'Forget it. I'm glad I found out exactly where I stand with you now, but there are more important issues here.'

She folded her hands tightly in her lap.

'You started to tell me why you suspect the fitness centre. Sit down. Here's your big chance to convince me. I want to hear exactly what you've discovered, and who else shares your ideas.'

He sat down.

'No-one else. I do know, however, when Sandon first experimented with drugs, he bought them from someone at the centre. He told me as much after he broke down and confessed he'd tried an illegal substance. He wouldn't say whom he bought them from, so I assumed it was some desperate addict hanging around the carpark. But talking to Kane the other day, I thought it significant that his father moved him from Brett Woods' squad to yours after Sandon's earlier flirtation with drugs.'

'It's ridiculous to suspect Brett Woods. He's a fitness fanatic.'

'Everyone working at the centre appears to be a fitness fanatic. In fact, some of those paid henchmen who hang around Connor look as if they have designer-induced muscles. And, have you ever really wondered how your boss turned the centre into a gold mine in such a short time? I'd love to get my hands on the financial records he keeps in his upstairs apartment, not to mention what goes on up there. My brother's dead, Tessa, because someone recognised his vulnerability and exploited it. I can't forget that. I can't get on with my life until I know the truth.'

Tessa heard the pain in his voice. If only she could comfort him, hold him, tell him everything would be all right. Nothing had changed between them, yet everything had changed. It wouldn't be all right while the doubt about the fitness centre stood between them and the truth about Sandon's death remained unresolved. She tried to think clearly.

'All right, tell me how I can help to clear up the matter.'

He reached across to her and she allowed him to take her hands in his.

'Are you sure you want to do this?'

'I won't be able to operate effectively in the centre until I know whether or not you're right. Tell me what you want from me.'

'It could be dangerous, if they think

you suspect anything. I can't involve you. You're too precious to me. You know that, don't you? If nothing positive comes out of this mess, at least I've met the woman of my dreams, and when it's over, I'm going to marry you. I'm going to insist you say yes.'

His words sent a wave of warmth through her, but it was too early to allow her feelings to influence her judgment, too early to work out exactly how she should respond to his assertions about the centre. She released her hands and stood up.

'It may never be over, but should it happen, I'll consider your proposal.'

She tried to sound light-hearted, though she longed to say yes, and to the devil with everything else, but she was still slightly bruised by the fact that he had not trusted her enough to confide his fears. As they returned into the house, she determined that the quickest and smartest way to discover the truth about the centre was to do a bit of probing herself. If there was anything to find, she was well-positioned to find it.

Taking her in his arms, he said softly, 'Tessa, for now, I think it's best we don't see each other. That way, you won't be involved. Nothing can happen to you.'

'But I want to be involved. I want to know.'

'Sorry, sweetheart, I do this alone.'

She could hear the regret in his voice, see it in his eyes, but she hushed the words with a kiss. And shrugging from his hold, his kiss still warm on her lips, she forced out her words.

'I hope you find the answers. Good-night, Rick.'

As he closed the front door, the house fell silent, felt empty, like her heart, but of one thing she was certain. She would go looking for answers herself. And tilting her chin, she assured herself she'd find them.

The day Tessa returned to work, she found Kane Fraser's father waiting for her in the reception area. Apprehensive, she beckoned him into the small office and closed the door.

'I thought it only fair to advise you that I'm transferring Kane to another pool,' he began.

Her heart did a peculiar flip.

'Oh, I'm disappointed. Kane's been applying himself very well after switching to my squad. I have high hopes for him in the state championships. May I ask your reasons?'

'It's got nothing to do with your coaching. Look, are we likely to be interrupted? This is confidential.'

She went across and locked the door.

'Please, we like to hear if clients have complaints. We may be able to address them to your satisfaction.'

'You won't change my mind. It was hushed up, but you're probably aware a few weeks before his death, Sandon Truscott was accused of drug taking.'

'I only found out recently. So what are you saying, Mr Fraser?'

'I haven't told another soul, not even his mother, but my boy admitted he experimented with Sandon. It was a huge shock, but I worked on him and to his credit, Kane saw the danger and pulled himself together. Then he came to me after young Truscott's death, worried, insisting Sandon could have died from drugs. I reassured him of the coroner's findings, but I've been troubled ever since. I know the kids bought the stuff at the centre, but Kane won't say any more. Scared, no doubt.'

He shifted his weight from one leg to the other.

'I always say, where's there's smoke, there's fire. I'm nervous. That's why I'm transferring Kane to another centre. I'm not prepared to take chances with my boy's future and his health. He started swimming originally because he's asthmatic.'

Tessa breathed quickly. She could no longer ignore what were rumours so far, no longer brush off Rick's suspicions. It was time for her to start opening her eyes, looking for signs.

'Do you have other evidence to support your concerns about the centre, anything which confirms or suggests the drugs came from here?'

'I've got my son's word, and his belief that Truscott was still experimenting. That's enough for me.'

'Mr Fraser, Kane's made some serious allegations, and I'd like to follow them through. If your son could name the person who sold him and Sandon the drugs, it might clear up everything straightaway. Let me talk to him. Sometimes kids respond better to outsiders.'

She looked intently at Fraser, but she received the answer she expected when he refused to meet her gaze.

'I don't want any more pressure on my son. When I walk out of here, I want my family to forget the whole episode. And I want you to forget we ever had this conversation. No disrespect to you, Miss . . . er . . . Tessa. You're very good with the youngsters. If you moved to another fitness centre, I'd be happy for Kane to rejoin your squad. As it is, my advice to you is, find yourself a job somewhere else. This place is up to no good. I'm sure of it.'

He strode to the door and stood there waiting for her to unlock it.

'I can't change your mind?'

She asked the question, uncertain that she wanted to change it anyway.

'Sorry. I've said my last word.'

He walked out and left her holding the door, staring after him, her mind spinning with possibilities.

Tessa went out to her car and dialled Bill McCormack's number on her mobile phone. He sounded as if he'd woken from a deep sleep when he answered. Tessa decided to be direct.

'Bill, I need to get into Darren's office without him knowing. He keeps records up there I want to check.'

'Sorry, love. No can do. I already told Rick that. I only get into the shed to clean by appointment with his henchmen. I reckon there's something fishy going on in there, but it's none of my business. And don't you make it yours either, love. If he wants to entertain women . . . '

Tessa thanked him and hung up, disappointed.

But soon a second idea came into her head. In the office, she glanced over the board on which the keys to the various areas hung. She hadn't really expected to find the key to Darren's upstairs unit, but she sighed with frustration anyway. If something illegal was happening up there at night, but she couldn't get in to check it out . . . the voices in her head erupted . . . why not monitor the traffic on the stairs leading off the basketball court to see who visited the apartment and when?

Should she let Rick know what she planned, just in case? It wasn't hard to decide. She checked the wall planner, saw that a college basketball game was in progress, and, reaching for the key to the cleaners' storeroom, slipped it into her pocket. Gathering up her diary, pencil in hand, she sauntered towards the basketball court, as if she had business to negotiate in the area.

With little or no input to team games, she rarely visited the indoor court, but having weaved her way through two-thirds of the basketball arena, she reached the recessed back stairs. She hadn't thought about it before, but now it seemed obvious the stairs were an extension to the original building, and anyone observing from beneath would be glaringly obvious through the step slats. She looked about her. Nowhere else to hide.

Her trainers trod lightly but quickly up the stairs. She'd almost reached the top when she heard the door off the landing open. Her heart pulsed erratically. Someone was coming through — a man. She didn't know him, but he was thirtyish, sported a wealth of muscles and a suntan in his shorts and T-shirt. A new weights' instructor? She invented a smile, and grasped the door so that it remained open.

'I'm looking for Darren. He's not in his unit, by any chance?'

'I wouldn't know,' he growled.

'You have a key?'

'No.'

He seemed uncomfortable, and pushed passed her, but she clung to the door and took a guess.

'Didn't you just come out of there?'

'Yeah. What's it got to do with you? I thought these stairs were closed to the public.'

Cool it, she cautioned herself, don't arouse his suspicions.

'You're right, the area is out of bounds, that's why I'm questioning you. I'm the assistant manager. Sorry if I sounded aggressive. If you've got a key, you're obviously permitted to go in. I'm anxious to talk to Darren. Was he in the apartment by any chance?'

She hoped her smile reassured him.

'I haven't got a key. We use a key card when he's there. I thought you woulda known that.'

'I meant a key card, of course.'

'I had to make some deliveries to his joint. He let me out and then locked up. I reckon he went into the gym.'

'Thanks,' she said, but he wasn't listening for he took the stairs in quick time without looking back.

Tessa wiped her brow, continued through the door, closing it quietly and stepped into the gloomy landing. Three doors led off a small lobby, one to Darren's unit on her left, a second ahead of her into the gymnasium, and to her right the third, called the cleaners' storeroom. It held her interest. Once it provided entry from the gymnasium to the changing-rooms and showers, but after renovations late last year, members now accessed them directly from the gymnasium.

At the time she'd questioned the need for the renovations but Darren had said with a grin he wanted to divert the sweaty traffic going by his unit into the showers. Along with the rest of the management team, she'd laughed. Now, unsettled, attuned to the crowd of doubts circling in her head, she realised it could have been to prevent gym members noticing who went into his unit.

Slipping the key she'd borrowed from reception into the lock of the unused door, she held her breath, listened for the sounds of anyone approaching. As the lock clicked, she exhaled a long breath and eased the door ajar, wide enough to squeeze through. Then pulling it shut behind her, she let out a second long sigh of relief.

The small annex smelled dusty, airless. Her nose itched. It had no windows, but a skylight gave light enough to ensure she didn't trip over the old cleaning equipment which had been stored there and forgotten. Next she checked that she could lock off entry to the shower rooms, and finally assessed the closet-sized area would afford her the secret observation point she needed to check the visitors to Darren's unit. If anything was going on, she estimated it would be after the centre closed or during six and seven in the evening, the short, slack time in the gym.

Tomorrow night, she decided, impatient, but circumspect. She needed to think out her plan, compose herself. Her heart on hold, she locked the door of the storeroom and retreated to the landing door. There, she received a huge setback. Unknown to her, someone had recently organised it to operate on a key card system, too. She'd have to go through the gym to the front stairs, risk being observed and asked awkward questions.

Shaky, but determined, she retraced her steps along the lobby, out into the gym and sought out one of the instructors.

'Greg, I've been looking for Darren. He's not in his unit. Have you seen him around?'

Her voice sounded unnaturally stilted, and her lips ached as she held her fake smile.

'He just left. I'm surprised you didn't pass him on the stairs.'

Her cheeks felt hot.

'I guess we're playing hide and seek.

Thanks, Greg, I'll track him down.'

Tessa hurried away, down the front stairs, and out into the sunny world. For the remainder of the morning, the key to the unused storeroom felt hot in her pocket. Its empty place on the rack seemed to leap out at her whenever she passed through the reception area. At twelve-thirty, she raced off to the Esplanade to have a copy key cut, and after returning, breathless, she replaced the borrowed key when no-one was about. Her next challenge was to think of a way to gain entry through the back landing stairs. In the end, she compromised.

The following afternoon at four, Tessa said a showy cheerio in the reception area.

'I'm off to shower and change and I'm out of here for a few hours. I'll be back at seven,' she said to those, including Darren, within hearing distance.

Strolling away to the staff changing-room, she filled in time, impatient for things to quieten down, for staff and members to drift off. Finally, with a towel draped casually over her shoulder, she returned to the front stairs, glanced around before taking them, her heart beating as fast as her legs carried her up the flight. Next, unseen, she had to negotiate the gymnasium. A glimpse inside told her only a few people remained. Hopefully, she could pass through unnoticed.

She'd decided not to return Rick's messages on her answering machine, lest she succumb to the temptation to confide her plans, but suddenly her heart began to leap and dance dangerously. She longed for his reassuring presence, to feel his strength by her side. Her determination to uncover the truth had fuzzed her thinking. The chances she was taking manifested themselves as troubling questions. Suppose someone had seen her on the stairs? Suppose she were discovered going into the disused storeroom? Suppose she found evidence that drugs were being sold from Darren's unit? There were a million-and-one sup-poses, none of them reassuring, but all compelling her forward.

At last, she stood before the door to the storeroom. Unlocking it with shaky hands, she slipped inside. Her legs felt rubbery. She needed to sit down, but there was no chair. Opening the access door to the changing-rooms, she hurried into the women's area, found a plastic chair and retreated with it. Sitting down, she took a long breath before changing into black tights and a long-sleeved top. Her eyes had grown used to the gloominess, but she needed her torch to check the time. Five-thirty.

She tried using the half hour she had to wait by exercising her tense muscles, rolling her shoulders, breathing deeply, imagining herself strolling along a lonely beach, but the lack of air, her adrenalin flow, won over commonsense, and soon she could think of nothing but the hours ahead. Setting up her small audio tape-recorder, she perched on the edge of the chair and eased the door slightly ajar. The shard of light enabled her to capture a narrow view of the door to Darren's unit. Risky, but necessary. And she waited.

Dear heaven, was that someone knocking on the door into the showers? Her heart leaped and her body went rigid as she held her breath. The seconds felt like hours, but the knocking ceased, the voices faded. She sank back into her chair, dragged breath back into her lungs, and resumed her wait.

At exactly six-ten, two young men, neither of whom she recognised, tapped on Darren's door, uttered a word she couldn't quite understand, and were admitted. They came out shortly afterwards, and disappeared in the direction of the back stairs. Then visitors came at ten-minute intervals. By now, Tessa thought she knew the password they used to gain entry to Darren's unit. With a troubled heart, she also thought she knew why they were there.

She risked a peep at her watch in torchlight. Another ten minutes until the seven o'clock members arrived and the centre started swinging again. Her limbs felt stiff with tension, her breathing shallow and her nose prickled. Twice she stifled a sneeze, but on the third occasion she lost the contest. She pushed the door to, to cushion the sound, but a breeze on the landing must have caught it, for it slammed shut.

'Oh, no!' she gasped in the gloomy darkness.

★ ★ ★

Rick was worried. He'd told Tessa he wouldn't be in touch while he continued his search for the truth about Sandon's death, but the urge to see her, to be with her was too much. When she didn't return his calls at the centre, he decided to drop by her home. But still he drew a blank.

He dialled the centre to discover

she'd left at four, due back at seven. Where was she? If anything had happened to her . . . He got into the car and headed for the fitness centre. Tessa would be there at seven, and he had to see her.

In a foul mood, he dragged his bag from the car and stormed towards the entrance, and got into an altercation with the receptionist because he couldn't find his membership pass.

'Call the boss,' he growled. 'He knows me.'

'He's retired to his unit.'

Finally, Rick tipped everything from his bag and found the card.

'I presume Tessa will be along to take the seven o'clock swimming squad,' he asked.

'I'm new here. You'll have to consult the white board,' she said.

'Thanks. I'll be in the gym.'

He checked the board, confirmed Tessa's programme and stretched his legs up the stairs, suddenly anxious to be there, to use the time in the gym to observe the instructors and their movements. People were drifting out of the area, only he was arriving. In the empty changing-room, he stripped, dragged on a singlet and brief shorts. As he came out, for a minute he thought he smelled a familiar fragrance. He also thought he saw a long-fingered hand wrapped around the door opposite, closing it.

He sniffed the air. The perfume lingered. Tessa? He spoke her name to himself. His fist came close to knocking on the door, but the voices in his head called for caution, persuaded him he'd let his imagination, his desire to see Tessa cloud his judgment. Other women probably used the same perfume. Other women had long-fingered, delicately-tanned hands. Earlier he'd wondered about that door and had made subtle enquiries. It was now unused but the room beyond still stored cleaning equipment and odd materials. Chances were the perfume belonged to a woman cleaner.

Unsettled, he stood in the entrance to the gym, glancing around. He noticed a running machine located so that when using it, if the door into the lobby were opened, one could view the access to Connor's unit. Dare he risk opening the door? Sure, he thought, why not? Connor's door would provide very interesting viewing. Strolling across, he clutched the handle, but the door wouldn't budge. Apparently it was locked from the other side.

He did a fifteen-minute work-out on the walking machine, trying to decide what to do next. Hang around up here until seven when he expected Tessa to arrive back at the centre, or wait in the carpark for her to arrive? Images of the door to the cleaning area and the long fingers he thought he'd seen kept flitting through his mind. It prompted interesting thoughts. Suppose that door could be opened. Suppose it gave access to the private area around Connor's unit.

He turned off the machine, mopped

his brow and made for the showers. No-one was around. He by-passed the showers, going straight to the cleaners' storeroom. It was locked.

After taking a quick shower, he dressed, bought coffee at a takeaway café, and retired to the carpark to wait for Tessa's arrival. But seven o'clock ticked over to seven-fifteen and she didn't come. Using his mobile, he phoned the centre.

'No, Tessa hasn't arrived,' he was told.

'Didn't she have a squad at seven?'

'Yes, but apparently she's not coming.'

'Someone phoned? Is she ill?'

'I can't help you there.'

Rick felt cold. A sense of foreboding engulfed him. He had to find her.

8

Rick switched on the car's ignition and crunched it into reverse. Someone was hammering on his window. It was Kane Fraser! He killed the engine and wound down the window.

'I'm in a hurry. What's the problem?' he asked the youngster.

Kane looked around him. Rick noticed a youth standing close by.

'Rick, I've been looking everywhere for you. We need to talk to you.'

'Can't it wait? Tessa's missing. I'm on my way around to her place now. If she's not there . . . '

He tried not to think about the answer, but more and more an idea was forming in his head. More and more he thought of the fragrance and the fingers, and that locked door outside the gym area.

'What do you mean, missing?' Kane said.

'She didn't turn up to work tonight and isn't answering her phone.'

'Why can't we talk while you drive around to her house?' Kane asked with quiet determination.

'OK, get in.'

The young men scrambled into the back seat.

'By the way, Rick, do you remember Jason? He was in the same squad with me and Sandy. You have something to tell Rick, don't you, Jase?'

As Rick drove from the carpark, his attention was suddenly focused. Could this be the breakthrough he'd been looking for?

'Yeah? I'm listening.'

Jason spoke for the first time.

'You won't mention my name? My mum'll kill me if she knows.'

Impatient, Rick snapped, 'Get on with it,' before softening his tone. 'Sorry, I'm just anxious. Look, I can't promise anything until I know what you have to say, but if it's about drug dealing at the centre, I have a score to settle. I promise I'll do my best to protect you.'

'Jase was offered drugs at one of the squad's parties, just like Sandy and me. I'm sorry I didn't say anything when it happened to us, and my dad came the heavy with me. Sandy might still be here. That's why, when Jase mentioned it, I persuaded him to talk to you.'

'Who offered the drugs?'

Rick's heart pumped wildly. He fought to keep his mind on the traffic.

'If you're sure I won't get into trouble . . . '

'Come on. You've come this far.'

'Our coach, Woodsy, took Rowan and me aside. We haven't been swimming very well lately. He told us he knew a way we could improve.'

Rick knew it. His gut instinct told him months ago Brett Woods had to be involved, and now he just might be able to nail the guy. But he didn't only want the middle man. He wanted the brains behind the heartless trade. He wanted that person exposed and the business closed down.

'You refused?'

'I was confused. My mum always gives me a hard time when I don't swim good times, but I knew it would be cheating. Anyway, Woodsy told us to think about it. My mate and I agreed to meet him tonight on the back stairs after the late squad. I don't want to go, but I've got this ache in the gut. He warned us not to say anything to anybody or we'd meet with an accident.'

Rick pulled the car into the kerbside outside Tessa's house.

'Jason, I appreciate what you've done in coming to me, and I promise you you'll be safe. But telling me isn't enough. Will you help me shut down this illicit trade and get the creeps operating it behind bars? You know they were responsible for my brother's death?'

'I dunno. I'm not like Sandy. The girls all liked him. I'm dull and . . . '

'Sandon's dead because he stupidly put winning and having a good time ahead of everything else. My fault, I reckon. Anyway, the point is you've done the right thing. But it's only the first step. More young fitness fanatics will have their lives ruined if we can't close down the trade. You do realise that? Someone has to have the courage to get the police the proof they need. You could be that person.'

'Nah, I couldn't. I haven't got the bottle.'

'Look, I'm going in to see if Tessa's home. You think about it. You could be a hero.'

Jason went pale.

'Hey, Rick,' Kane called, as he got out of the car, 'I've just thought about it. My dad went to see Tessa. He told her I said me and Sandy got the drugs at the centre. Do you reckon her disappearance could have something to do with that?'

'We'll cross that bridge when we come to it,' Rick replied.

He strode through the gate, up the path, calling Tessa's name, fear gripping his heart. He didn't want to alarm the kids, especially Jason. He needed him to feel worthwhile, positive, but Rick sensed she wouldn't be here. Somehow, he knew she'd been locked in that cleaners' room. Was she still there?

The silent house mocked him. He forced open a back window and climbed in. There was no sign of Tessa. He listened to her answering machine. Nothing useful there so he returned to the car.

'I have to make one more phone call,' he said to the two lads.

He asked to be put through to Bill McCormack, and Bill confirmed what he feared. Yes, Tessa did seek his help to get into Connor's pad, but he told her to forget it. Clearly she hadn't taken his advice. Rick tried not to sound over-anxious, conscious not to alarm the easily-intimidated Jason.

'Tessa's not home, and apparently she's been doing a bit of detective work on her own. Look, I need your help more than ever. We have to find Tessa. What time did Brett Woods say he'd meet you at the centre?'

'Five after ten, eh, Jase?' Kane answered. 'You're gonna do what Rick wants, aren't you? If anything's happened to Tessa . . . '

'What will it take?' Jason asked in a subdued voice.

'Good man,' Rick said. 'We'll have to talk to the police, but here's what I propose . . . '

★ ★ ★

'That blasted woman,' Connor snarled to his two henchmen. 'She's pushed her way into my affairs once too often. Did you let reception know she wouldn't be around for a bit and get someone to take her squad?'

'Done.'

'OK. We'll get that room boarded up next week. Our amateur sleuth has stuck her pretty little nose into my business for the last time. But I'm not giving her the satisfaction of knowing for sure I'm involved in the trade.'

'So what do you want us to do with her?'

'I don't know what she's found out, but even if she's only suspicious, I can't take the risk. I suggest a road accident. Her mother died recently. She doesn't turn up to work, gets someone to phone in for her. She's depressed, driving dangerously at night along the beach road to the Point, her car goes over the edge. That should do it. It'll be worth your while. No slip ups.'

'Gotcha, boss. When?'

'You sure she can't escape? She's fit and strong, remember.'

'No way. Mr Australia couldn't burst out of those ropes.'

'Better get it over before daylight. Once her body's found we'll have the media nosing around the place. I need time to close down our profitable little sideline here for a few weeks.'

He laughed.

'Later we can reassess the situation. I've been thinking about reintroducing the availability of the new drug that proved fatal to that cocky young swimmer a while back. I'll alert Woodsy when he gets here tonight not to sell anything to his squad for a while. Send the weights' contacts in after you leave. I want everything off my premises before our pushy, little assistant manager meets her fate.'

He laughed again.

'Such a pity she didn't learn not to mess with me.'

* * *

Tessa urged herself not to faint, but the airless room, the gag in her mouth, the ropes binding her to the chair had sapped her energy. She thought of Bill. If he heard she was missing, he might remember their conversation about trying to get into Darren's room and put two and two together. He was her only hope. She wriggled vigorously in her chair, wondered if the rope around her wrists might not be a little loser.

Think positive. That's what her mother would have advised. Rick filled her thoughts. If only she hadn't been so independent. If she'd trusted him, taken him into her confidence, she wouldn't be in this situation. What if she never saw him again? What if they didn't get their chance at happiness together? And she'd never get to tell him the answer to the cryptic clue he posed on that first day! A gentle smile touched her lips.

She imagined Rick slamming through the door, calling her name, taking her in his arms. She felt the warmth of his lips against her cheek, the dampness of hot tears, his hand caressing her hair, his eyes reassuring her she was safe, would always be safe with him. She hung on to the dream, until reality got in the way. She shivered. She didn't need to be a rocket scientist to know Connor couldn't afford to keep her alive.

Her struggles tipped over the chair and it crashed to the ground. As she passed out, she thought, surely someone had missed her when she didn't turn up to the evening squad . . .

It was exactly five past ten when Jason and Rowan stood at the foot of the back stairs of the fitness centre. Jason looked anxiously about him.

'Where's Woodsy? He's late,' he whispered.

'He'll be here, mate. Calm down.'

'I don't like this.'

They heard a sound above them, footsteps. Woodsy appeared on the staircase.

'I'm glad you kids made the right decision. You're winners already. Our squad's gonna be the top in the state. Come on up, fellas.'

Rowan pushed Jason ahead of him. Jason's legs felt wobbly. He clutched the rail, impelled himself upward one step at a time, telling himself he had to make it. Another five, maybe ten minutes and it would all be over. He'd never step inside this place again, never swim another lap, he thought. He'd make his mum understand that there was more to life than being a sporting icon. He wanted to be an engineer.

Suddenly he found himself at the top of the stairs, saw Woodsy insert a key card, the door swing open. Yikes, could they hear his heart pounding?

★   ★   ★

The innocuous-looking blue van sat in the shadows of the trees lining the perimeter of the carpark. Inside the cabin, crowded with three men and an array of listening equipment, Rick, who had persuaded the police in the drug squad to let him sit in, sat stiffly, alert. He recognised Jason's voice, weak, anxious.

Speak up, kid, let's hear it loud and clear, he urged silently.

They'd been let into the Connor unit now. Woodsy was doing all the talking. Where the devil was that slippery swine,

Connor? Rick wanted him.

'The deal's about to take place.'

The detective spoke into an inter-com, instructing the uniformed personnel secretly positioned outside the centre.

'Go, go, go.'

Rick wrenched open the door of the van, cursing that he'd been forbidden to wait closer to the centre. Racing towards the building, it became achingly clear to him that nailing the drug dealers now held second place in importance in his life. Finding Tessa, making her safe, was his most important priority.

Arriving at the basketball arena, breathless, he found the landing door had been forced open. On a second wind, he took the back stairs with giant strides. On the landing, Connor was being led from his unit, his hands cuffed at his back.

'You rotten swine,' Rick spat at him. 'Where is she? What've you done with her?'

'Tessa? Nothing, old man, but I

heard a whisper she's been depressed. Perhaps she's had an accident.'

His cool, smooth manner, the sarcastic curl of his lips, upped Rick's anger. Rick cursed himself for a fool. He should have barged in hours ago, found Tessa, instead of waiting those long hours for the drug raid. If he'd lost her, he could only blame himself.

'Ignore rubbish like him,' he ranted. 'What's happened to Tessa?'

But the police didn't even look up. They had their hands full with arrests, searching the premises for evidence. Handcuffed, Brett Woods emerged next from the unit, his muscled body now bowed. Rick confronted him.

'You killed my brother. I hope you rot.'

Woods stumbled then raised his head.

'I had no idea some people could be sensitive to the drug. If it's any consolation, I'm truly sorry.'

'But it hasn't stopped you recruiting more vulnerable young kids, has it?

You're scum, mate. Here's your big chance to show some genuine remorse. What's happened to Tessa? Where have they taken her?'

The police escorts forced Rick back, but Woods started to blabber.

'It's not too late. It wasn't going to happen until early tomorrow morning. I wasn't going to let it happen, anyway. I planned to make an anonymous call to the cops. She's around here somewhere.'

Rick's heart leaped with hope.

'Yeah? Who do you think you're kidding? You weren't going to tell anyone. You're a bully and a coward, mate, but thanks for the information. I think I know where she is.'

Two strides on and he pounded on the door of the storeroom, calling Tessa's name. Pressing his ear to it, he listened, his body tense for her answer, for some sign that she was in there. But he couldn't hear anything.

'Damn it, will you keep the noise down!' he shouted in frustration into the confusion in the passageway, but no-one heard.

He could wait no longer. Seizing a detective by the arm, he swung him around.

'Get her out. She may have been in there for hours. Get her out now, before it's too late.'

The heavy police rammer took only seconds to crash open the door. They found Tessa on the floor. Kneeling, Rick felt her pulse. Positive! The tension in his body eased as he gathered her in his arms.

'I thought I'd lost you,' he murmured over and over.

Tessa opened her eyes and blinked. It was exactly as she dreamed it. Rick had come to her rescue.

She smiled gently as he paused to right the chair, to untie her with strong hands, and again she felt his arms, her head against his chest. She heard his heart pounding, or was it her own? Two hearts beating as one.

'What took you so long?' she asked,

as he carried her from her prison, down the front stairs and into the staff-room, where he laid her on the couch.

Kneeling beside it, he brushed her hair back from her face.

'I can't believe you're safe. I've got you back. If you've never seen a guy cry . . . '

He brushed at his eyes, misty with tears.

'You should be weeping, not me, sweetheart,' he apologised. 'You're the one who's been to hell and back. I'm the fool who didn't act fast enough.'

'Did I ever mention how much I admire men who aren't too macho to cry?' she whispered.

Her voice broke then and she could no longer hold back her tears.

'That's good because you're stuck with him now.'

Rick ran the back of his hand across his eyes. She moved to sit up, to tell him she was fine and wanted to go home, but she crashed back on to the sofa again.

'My body aches all over,' she said, stifling a second burst of crying.

Rick found some towels, folded them behind her head and eased it back.

'Better?' he asked.

She nodded. Sensitively he lifted her wrist and massaged the ugly red mark left by the ropes. His touch eased the pain.

'When can we go home?' she asked.

'I can't promise anything. I want the police doctor to check you over as soon as he's free upstairs. You may need to go to the hospital for a thorough check-up, and the police will want to talk to you.'

'But not tonight,' she said, her fingers reaching out to touch his very dear, but strained face. 'I'm going to be all right, Rick. Independent women don't cave in easily.'

'Independent women sometimes get more than they bargained for.'

His strong but gentle hands transferred to her other wrist.

'If that includes being rescued by a

handsome knight who's swapped his armour for a track-suit, I can hack it.'

Tessa managed a laugh. The nightmare was almost over.

9

After an overnight stay in hospital, Tessa was allowed home, and there, with Rick by her side, she answered the repetitive and lengthy questioning of the detectives.

'How could they think I was involved?' she said crossly after they'd left. 'I was bound and locked up for hours. Do they think I arranged that for myself?'

'Don't excite yourself, sweetheart. They had to explore all possibilities,' Rick assured her gently.

'Rick Tremaine, I know you think I should have twigged to it, that I was blind to what was happening right under my nose.'

She dropped her irritated tone, listened to her own words and for the first time she could see how it might look to others.

'Maybe I was,' she said slowly. 'I loved my job, the contact with people. I saw only what I wanted to. I knew Darren was a lecher, a self-opinionated, obnoxious creature, yet it didn't occur to me he could be a drug dealer, even when you hinted at it.'

'Hush now. You weren't the only one who didn't know what was going on, and at least when you had your suspicions you did something. People like Fraser walked away.'

'People do that. They put their families first. It's not hard to understand,' she replied.

'All I can say is, thank goodness Connor and his associates will pay for their sins.'

Rick poured champagne, handed Tessa a glass, and joined her on the sofa. The two flutes clinked musically together.

'To us,' he said.

'To you and me,' Tessa echoed, 'and to finally hearing your version of how you nabbed the crooks and single-handedly organised the biggest drug bust in years, according to the media.'

He laughed.

'You can't believe everything you read. The kids actually came to me before they knew you were missing. Kane and Jason are the heroes, especially Jason. It took every ounce of guts for him to walk into Connor's place wearing a police wire. There were times as the police tracked him into the centre and up those stairs when I thought he'd blow it or turn and run, and I wouldn't have blamed him. He's not by nature an out-going, headstrong boy.'

Tessa looked up, saw the pain of remembrance flicker in his eyes.

'Not like Sandon?'

'No, not like my brother. He was bright, full of fun on the outside, but inside, screwed up, I think.'

'You're not still blaming yourself, Rick?'

'I'm working my way through it, but it still hurts. I realise now that lots of kids do things to please their parents when it's not what they really want. Kane wanted to talk to you, but his father said no, and I bet you didn't know young Jason hates competitive swimming. He's doing it to please his mother. She's the one who wants medals, not him. He'd settle for being an engineer. I've told her I'll take him on at my place during holidays and weekends while he goes to university, if she agrees.'

Tessa placed her half-empty glass on a side table and edged closer to him. There was so much to love about this man.

'It's an offer no woman could refuse her son. After all, Jason's a big man now in the eyes of his peers.'

'Have you thought about what you might do?' he asked.

'As a matter of fact, I had a phone call today. The owner of Work Out, Joe Cotchin, is closing it down. He asked me to manage his new health and fitness centre down the coast. It would mean leaving town.'

Rick looked startled.

'It's a good offer.'

'I was hoping for a better one, from you. You did say . . . '

She smiled coquettishly.

'You mean, when it was all over I'd insist you marry me? But I wouldn't stand in the way of a career move like that.'

'You wouldn't be standing in my way, Rick. I've already found a position as physical education instructor at the local secondary school, and the public pool nearby is looking for a part-time swimming teacher. If you still want me . . . '

She picked up his arm, placed it around her shoulders and nestled into his chest.

'But would that satisfy you?'

'For goodness' sake, Rick, will you ask me to marry you, or do I have to ask you? On that chance encounter in the café, I decided you were a fast worker. It seems I was mistaken. Which reminds me, I don't think I told you the answer to the cryptic crossword clue you gave me that day. So much has happened I kept forgetting.'

'Don't eat so quickly, that was the clue, wasn't it? As I remember, you couldn't work it out.'

'Of course I could. Think I'm dumb or something? The answer was 'fast'. Not to eat is to fast, and doing something quickly could be fast. You see, not just a pretty face.'

Her lips brushed against his cheek. He smiled, his eyes gleaming. He tilted her chin in his hand.

'I can't let a bright girl like you slip through my fingers, can I? Tessa, will you marry me?'

'Yes,' she whispered. 'I couldn't give up the chance of growing old with someone who's into cryptics. I should warn you, I've been studying them ever since, and I'm a pretty fast learner!'

We do hope that you have enjoyed reading this large print book.

Did you know that all of our titles are available for purchase?

We publish a wide range of high quality large print books including:
Romances, Mysteries, Classics
General Fiction
Non Fiction and Westerns

Special interest titles available in large print are:
The Little Oxford Dictionary
Music Book, Song Book
Hymn Book, Service Book

Also available from us courtesy of Oxford University Press:
Young Readers' Dictionary
(large print edition)
Young Readers' Thesaurus
(large print edition)

For further information or a free brochure, please contact us at:
Ulverscroft Large Print Books Ltd.,
The Green, Bradgate Road, Anstey,
Leicester, LE7 7FU, England.
Tel: (00 44) 0116 236 4325
Fax: (00 44) 0116 234 0205

VISIONS OF THE HEART

Christine Briscomb

When property developer Connor Grant contracted Natalie Jensen to landscape the grounds of his large country house near Ashley in South Australia, she was ecstatic. But then she discovered he was acquiring — and ripping apart — great swathes of the town. Her own mother's house and the hall where the drama group met were two of his targets. Natalie was desperate to stop Connor's plans — but she also had to fight the powerful attraction flowing between them.

DIVIDED LOYALTIES

Phyllis Demaine

When Heather's fiancé, Adrian, is offered a wonderful job in America their future seems rosy. However, Adrian's brother, Carl, a widower, asks for Heather's help with his small, deaf son. Help which, as a speech therapist, Heather is qualified to give. But things become complicated when Carl goes abroad on business and returns with Gisel, to whom his son takes an instant dislike. This puts Heather in the position of having to choose between the boy's happiness and her own.